B
DO NO
BO
BEGIN

Hey! You'd never noticed that comic shop before. It's kind of dusty — but man, does it have great comics!

If you check out the books on the spinner rack, you're spun into a comic-book universe. Which superhero do you want to be? Will the supervillains destroy you? Or worse — will you end up as an ink blot?

If you follow the HORROR sign to the basement, look out! You'll find horror down there, all right. But not horror *comics*. . .

This scary adventure is all about you. You decide what will happen. And you decide how terrifying the scares will be!

Start on *PAGE 1.* Then follow the instructions at the bottom of each page. *You* make the choices. If you choose well, you'll make it home again. But if you make the wrong choice . . . BEWARE!

SO TAKE A DEEP BREATH. CROSS YOUR FINGERS. AND TURN TO PAGE 1 TO *GIVE YOURSELF GOOSEBUMPS!*

READER BEWARE —
YOU CHOOSE THE SCARE!

Look for more
GIVE YOURSELF GOOSEBUMPS adventures
from R.L. STINE

1 Escape From the Carnival of Horrors
2 Tick Tock, You're Dead!
3 Trapped in Bat Wing Hall
4 The Deadly Experiments of Dr Eeek
5 Night in Werewolf Woods
6 Beware of the Purple Peanut Butter
7 Under the Magician's Spell
8 The Curse of the Creeping Coffin
9 The Knight in Screaming Armour
10 Diary of a Mad Mummy
11 Deep in the Jungle of Doom
12 Welcome to the Wicked Wax Museum
13 Scream of the Evil Genie
14 The Creepy Creations of Professor Shock
15 Please Don't Feed the Vampire!
16 Secret Agent Grandma

Little Comic Shop of Horrors

R.L. Stine

SCHOLASTIC

Scholastic Children's Books
Commonwealth House, 1–19 New Oxford Street, London WC1A 1NU, UK
a division of Scholastic Ltd
London ~ New York ~ Toronto ~ Sydney ~ Auckland
Mexico City ~ New Delhi ~ Hong Kong

First published in the USA by Scholastic Inc., 1997
First published in the UK by Scholastic Ltd, 2000

ISBN 0 439 99516 7

Typeset by Rowland Phototypesetting Ltd, Bury St Edmunds, Suffolk
Printed by Cox & Wyman Ltd, Reading, Berks.

10 9 8 7 6 5 4 3 2 1

"I thought after-school clubs were supposed to be fun," you grumble. You love comic books. And a comic club sounded cool. But it's run by Horace Grumbacher, the dullest kid in school!

How could someone make a subject like comics boring?

Horace manages.

He clicks his slide projector to a picture of a comic-book cover. "Here's the first issue starring Super-Doer," he drones. "Today, it's worth nearly two hundred *thousand* dollars."

Click! "And here's the first appearance of Ballistic Bug. This comic goes for nearly twenty thousand."

As if any kid in this club can afford that, you think.

The projector clicks again, and a horror comic appears on the screen. Excellent! You love horror!

But Horace can even make horror dull. "This issue of *The Cellar of Scary Stories* went for sixteen hundred dollars," he lectures.

An ugly face sneers at you from the comic cover. Yuck! It looks like a rotten pumpkin. With warts.

You turn away, and notice the classroom clock. How did it get so late? You run outside — in time to see a horrible sight.

"Oh, *no*!" you groan.

What's wrong? Find out on PAGE 2.

The school bus is already a block away. It left without you!

"Thanks a lot, Horace," you growl. Because of his boring lecture, now you have to walk home!

If you follow the same route as the bus, you won't get home for hours. You decide you'd better try a short cut. Even though it means going through a part of town you've never seen before.

You walk and walk along your short cut. With every step you take, your book bag gets heavier.

The area you're cutting through looks a little weird. The buildings are all old and dingy. The shops huddle together as if they're holding each other up.

And the stuff in the windows is *very* weird. You pass a clothes shop that seems to be selling Halloween costumes — even though Halloween is months away. And those dolls in that toy-shop window. They look like . . . vampires!

You're relieved when you spot a shop for vacuum cleaners. *That's* normal, you think. And next to it. . .

Hey! A comic shop!

Want to visit? Go to PAGE 3.

You step inside. The comic shop is dimly lit. You can barely make out the comics on spinning racks. Beyond, in deeper shadows, are tables with row after row of boxes. These are the back issues, where collectors look for treasures.

The owner stands behind a cash register. He looks familiar, with his round face and warts. But you can't place him.

He grunts when he sees you. "Humph. Kids."

Well, who does he expect to come in and buy comics?

As you walk past him, the shop owner calls out, "Leave your bag up here!"

You scowl. Why is he treating you like a thief? You think about leaving. But you'd like a rest from walking. And besides, you really want to check out the comics.

Strolling round the racks, you notice the latest issue of *Major Disaster.* You bought it just a week ago. This guy has a sticker on it for half price!

Walking a little faster, you start picking up comic books. Doesn't the owner know what these things are worth?

The deeper into the shop you go, the darker it gets. A pair of bookcases block your way. But there's a little space between them. You see light coming through the crack. . .

Push through to PAGE 4.

You squeeze between the bookcases into an open area. A dusty light bulb dangles from the ceiling. In its dim glow, you make out another spinning rack full of comics.

A sign taped to the top of the rack says:

YOU THINK THIS IS A LIBRARY?
LOOK, BUT DON'T TOUCH . . . OR YOU'LL BE SORRY.

You peer at the comics on the rack. Whoa — that's the issue of Ballistic Bug from Horace's slide show! The comic is marked for two bucks! And up there, on the top rack — is that the incredibly expensive copy of Super-Doer?

Then you notice something else. A doorway. Beyond the rack. Metal stairs lead downwards — to the basement, you guess. An arrow-shaped sign points down the stairway. It reads: HORROR.

There's also a tattered sign on the open door. You try to make out the faded letters. It seems to say NO ADMITTANCE. TRESPASSERS WILL BE GLOMPFed.

GLOMPFed? What's that?

You don't really care. All you care about is making a tough decision: should you take a closer look at the rack, or should you go down to the horror section?

If you check out the rack, turn to PAGE 12.
If you go downstairs, turn to PAGE 51.

A way out?

"Count me in!" you shout. Your heart starts to thump in your chest. There might be a way out of this maze of horrors!

Then you start to wonder. Why is Russell treating it like a deep, dark secret?

Russell sees the look on your face and explains.

"We're not taking the whole group — only a few. I don't want to raise people's hopes. Besides, it will be safer this way."

"Safer?" you gulp. Taking a small group through a maze full of killer creatures doesn't sound safe to you. You'd be happier in a large group — say, an army.

Why does Russell think only a handful of people would be better?

When you ask, Russell replies, "I don't want to draw attention to us — either from the guy upstairs, or from the maze creatures. They'd be sure to spot a big crowd passing through their hunting grounds." Russell shakes his head. "And that would be bad, because where we're going is the most dangerous part of the maze!"

Find more good news on PAGE 29.

Shuddering, you follow Bob. The angry hissing of the snake-creature fades. But you find yourself glancing back every few steps. Anything that sounds like a scrape freezes your blood. You don't want to see that thing ever again!

All too soon, Bob halts.

"Wait here," he says, pointing to a doorway. "I'll get Russell."

"Who's Russell?" you ask. "And why do I have to wait?"

"Russell is our leader," Bob replies. "He decides whether or not you can join us. Until then, you're not allowed in our camp."

He looks you over again. "Don't worry, though. I think you're just what we need."

Bob goes off, leaving you by the doorway.

This is great, you think. You're lost in a maze where giant snake-monsters rule. And now you have to wait! Alone!

Or do you?

If you follow Bob, turn to PAGE 131.
If you obey him and wait, turn to PAGE 20.

You dash out to the street, shouting for help. A block away, you find two police officers. They give you funny looks as you tell them what happened. But they follow you to the shop.

"Here's the place," you exclaim, leading them to the Comics Dungeon. Hey, that's weird! The place is locked up.

Through the window, you see only an empty, dusty shop. It looks as if it's been vacant for months!

A neighbouring shop owner has the key. A search shows the place is bare. No Milo. No comics. No cellar!

"I was there! I was!" you insist.

The police don't believe you. But when you step outside, you spot Jack and Cammie, looking dazed. One officer stares. "I know those kids! They disappeared a couple of weeks ago."

In the next few days, dozens of lost kids turn up all over town. None of them seem to remember where they've been.

No one believes your story. You start to doubt it yourself. Until you find the comic you stuffed in your pocket. It's the first issue of Super-Doer. The one from Horace's slide show.

Okay, so people don't believe your story. But they have to believe the mansion you bought after you sold your rare comic book for loads of money. . .

THE END

8

You reach into your pocket and grab your keys. They're the sharpest things you have on you.

Then, lowering your head, you charge! You hold your arm straight out, with the longest key jutting out of your fist. "Die, Monster!" you yell.

Quivering purple flesh quakes in front of you. You ram into it at full speed.

But King Jellyjam's body doesn't pop like a balloon. It just gives way, then bounces back. You're sent flying — until you're caught in a giant hand.

"Die? Is that what you said?" Milo's voice asks.

The hand brings you high over the hideous purple face. Rubbery lips open to reveal big, stained yellow teeth. Two pink tongues waggle at you as the hand lets go.

"Fire. Maybe I should have tried fire," you think as you drop into the huge, hungry mouth.

THE END

All of you hurry on fearfully. The snuffly noise fades away. After several more twists and turns, you find a long, straight hallway. At the end are three openings.

"Watch out for traps," Jack whispers. "I'll take the left. Cammie gets the middle. You take the right."

Sneaking down the hall, you peer through your doorway. Hey! This must be the storeroom for the comic shop upstairs. It's packed with hundreds of boxes of comic books!

Then Cammie calls excitedly, "In here — quick!"

You and Jack join her in a room that's very different from the rest of the maze. It has wall-paper and a rug. A reading lamp stands beside a big armchair. There's a bed in the corner.

And there's a full-length mirror in an old-fashioned frame against one wall. Cammie steps up to it — and the mirror begins to glow! She sticks out her hand.

It sinks right in!

"A magic mirror!" you cry. "Maybe it's the way out!"

Cammie stands frozen in front of the mirror. Should you let her try to step through? Or will you push in first?

If you let Cammie go, turn to PAGE 118.
If you push ahead, try PAGE 78.

10

No time to worry about where you're going. You leap into a tornado of light. It whirls around you, faster and faster. Your body stretches like toffee. . .

Then, with a *SNAP!* you're back to normal.

You're in sunshine, in the middle of a street. A horn blares behind you as a school bus screeches to a halt.

Wait a minute. It's not just *any* school bus. It's *your* school bus. The one you missed at the start of this strange adventure!

"I would've stopped," the annoyed bus driver tells you. "You didn't have to get yourself almost run over."

You climb aboard, clutching your school books. Where did they come from? You don't know. And what happened to Dr Doof? Certainly, there's no sign of him here.

A breeze blows a piece of paper through the bus window. It's a page from a comic. It has only one large panel.

A chill runs down your spine when you see the picture. It shows a horrified Dr Doof, frozen in the act of jumping through a hole in space. . .

THE END

You form a plan. You just hope you're right!

A slimy, purple hand grabs you. "Answer me!" Milo's voice gurgles out of King Jellyjam's body. "Am I scary enough?"

Tears run down your face from his stench. You raise a hand to your ear. "Eh?" you ask. "What's that, you say?"

The creature's watery yellow eyes bulge out in fury. "Am I scary enough for you?" the awful voice roars.

The smell is growing even worse. You choke and cough. But you manage to gasp, "You'll have to speak up."

Milo sucks in a huge breath to yell at you. Snails rattle to the floor as his body swells. His hand squeezes you painfully.

Then it loosens. The yellow eyes cross. King Jellyjam's body topples with a *splat*!

You got it right! In the book, King Jellyjam was suffocated by his own stink! You made it happen!

It seems that the end of Milo means the end of his magic maze too. The walls shimmer and melt, revealing a cave. Not far away, a set of stairs leads upwards — towards light.

You start climbing. You just want to go home. Get some rest. Recover from your incredible adventure.

And take a bath! You stink!

THE END

12

You've got to see if that two-dollar comic is really the famous first issue of Super-Doer. But when you grab the spinner rack, it starts to turn — by itself! Still worse, the metal rack seems to have glued itself to your hand. You can't let go!

Your jaw drops as the moving rack yanks you off your feet. You're dragged round in a circle. And the rack keeps speeding up.

Soon, to your horror, you can't touch the floor any more. It's like some sort of weird carnival ride. The rack is whizzing round, and you're flying through the air!

"Hey! Hey, mister!" you yell to the shop owner. But the words are torn from your lips by a screaming wind. You feel as if you're caught in a tornado.

You clench your teeth to keep from groaning. Your body is stretched out, like you're a warm piece of toffee. You shift your grip. One hand touches a comic on the rack.

The comic starts to glow. Now, suddenly, there's a new pull.

You're being sucked into the glowing comic!

Fly to PAGE 103.

Dr Doof wags an armoured finger at you. “You should have figured it out yourself. Whenever my blast-bolts hit your Insecto-Electric Hornet’s Sting, there’s a brief tesseract reaction.”

“A *what*?” you ask.

“A hole in space,” Doof explains. “If we fire at each other at close range, and I heterodyne my blast-bolts —”

“In English, please,” you say as politely as you can.

“And little words, no doubt,” Dr Doof huffs. “All right. We’ll make a hole in space — and step through.”

Whatever.

“Let’s do it!” you cry.

You stand face to face with Dr Doof, readying your weapons. “On three,” Doof calls. “One, two. . .”

BABOOOOOM!

When your eyes finally clear, a shimmering black hole floats between you and Dr Doof.

Dr Doof suddenly leaps into the hole.

“Wait!” you cry. Where does he think he’s going?

And then you hear him scream!

If you follow Dr Doof, turn to PAGE 10.
If you look before you leap, turn to PAGE 90.

You're going to fight! Even though it takes all your courage just to gaze at Milo's new, rubbery face.

You try to remember the story you read. The girl who told the story managed to defeat King Jellyjam. But how? Terror has got your mind all mixed up.

Did she push King Jellyjam into an oven? No, that was the ending to an old fairy tale.

The gross purple face snorts at you. Your stomach gurgles at the sour stink of bad breath. Is that what destroyed King Jellyjam? Did he suffocate from his own smell?

Think! How would you destroy a huge purple body? One that looks just like a slime-filled *balloon*? Did the girl in the story poke King Jellyjam so he popped?

Those big yellow eyes are getting a nasty look. Time to decide!

Do you poke King Jellyjam? Turn to PAGE 8.

Do you try to suffocate the giant creature? Turn to PAGE 11.

When you shout the magic words, the universe does another quick change. You spin through the air. Incredible brightness glares around you. Then you thud to the floor.

You shake your head to clear your brain. You seem to be on a stage. You must be in an old theatre, or something. The blazing light comes from the fist of a man wearing black armour, goggles and a metal face mask.

It's Dr Doof! One of the greatest mad scientists in comics! He's also Ballistic Bug's worst enemy.

And right now he's aiming his armoured fists at *you*. Uh-oh! That means he's going to zap you with a blast-bolt!

Your brain is frozen with fear, so your body takes over on instinct. The gentle hum you've been noticing in the background rises into a frantic whine. Then you take off in flight!

Hey! How'd you do that?

Find out on PAGE 81.

You jump back with a horrified scream. These creatures aren't human! They're . . . bugs!

Oddly enough, when they see you, the bug-people leap back too. They raise sticklike arms in front of their faces. Their buzzing suddenly becomes very shrill.

I must look as scary to them as they do to me! you realize. Fighting back your own terror, you manage a friendly smile. What do good aliens say in sci-fi comics? Oh, right.

"I come in peace," you call.

Too bad the bug-people don't speak English. Their buzzing rises to a shriek as you walk towards them. You grab your ears at the shrill sounds of hundreds of alien screams. It's worse than the whine of a dentist's drill!

Ouch! Go to PAGE 93.

You turn anxiously to the rest of Y's Guys. Wolfen-Bean, the Fighting Vegetable and Stinky Stanley look confused. So does Jean Greene. You're not sure what her power is, but you know it involves coming back from the dead.

They're all fierce fighters. What will they do if they discover *you're* the alien Professor Y is talking about?

"Can you tell us more about these visitors?" you ask.

"Yeah, professor," Jean Greene pipes up. "How do we know they're evil?"

"Sure," Wolfen-Bean chimes in. "Maybe they're just lost, or something."

"This isn't something to vote over," Professor Y growls. "My marvellous mind powers warn me of danger." He closes his eyes as though he's listening to a tiny voice.

Then his eyes open wide. "One of the invaders is in this very room! It must be a shape-shifter!"

"Um, professor," you begin.

Professor Y whips around, pointing. "*You're* the one!"

Find out who he's pointing at on PAGE 134.

A big gob of goo flies from the creature's mouth. It misses you, but lands on the wall behind you. Immediately, the plywood starts to bubble and hiss! The thing's spit must be acid! If it had touched you. . .

"Run!" Russell shouts.

Alicia drags you round the corner. After a couple of minutes of running, the group slows down. "It's dangerous, but it's not fast," Alicia pants.

Ahead, Russell and Bob are arguing in whispers. Russell turns to all of you. "The Spitter is blocking the path we planned to take," he explains. "I think we should circle round it even though that means spending more time in the Danger Zone." He points at a doorway in the plywood wall. "But Bob thinks we can cut through here. The problem is, none of us have been through this part of the maze before."

Russell looks at your little group. "We'll take a vote. Which way do you want to go?"

If you go along with Russell, turn to PAGE 24.

If you think Bob has a better idea, turn to PAGE 128.

I hope I'm doing the right thing, you think. Wings buzzing, you flash towards the Doorway to Anywhere.

Darkness swallows you up. You feel a terrible chill. Invisible forces seize your body and hurl you through the blackness.

And then . . . the blackness isn't so total. In fact, it's more like grey. You're in a large, shadowy room. Near by, you see a spinner rack full of comics.

The doorway to anywhere has dumped you back in the comic shop where it all started!

Your wings buzz with joy —

Wings?

Hey! You're still Ballistic Bug! You still have your superpowers!

Excellent!

You fly to the front of the shop to confront the weird-looking man behind the counter. This is his shop, after all. Whatever is going on, he must know about it. And you've got a lot of questions you want answered!

Charge onwards to PAGE 76.

You wait for a long time. Just when you're about to give up and wander off, Bob returns with another older boy. "This is Russell," he says.

The big boss is tall and skinny, with thick glasses. As he gazes down at you, you're reminded of a stork you once saw in a zoo.

Russell bursts into a big smile. "Perfect, Bob!" he exclaims. "Just the right size."

You don't like the sound of that. Your Uncle Mel always says the same thing about the turkey at Thanksgiving dinner. "What am I perfect for?" you demand.

"I can't tell you — yet," Russell says mysteriously. "Anyway, I've got to test you first."

"*Test* me?" you cry in disbelief.

"Yes," Russell goes on. "I want you to bend your right leg up till you can catch hold of your ankle with your right hand."

"Are you serious?" you demand.

"Totally," Russell replies. "Do it, or you don't get in."

You heard Russell. Standing on one leg, bend your right foot back and try to catch your ankle.

If you succeed, turn to PAGE 79.

If you fail, turn to PAGE 133.

"I'm there!" you call, sloshing through the puddle. The mystery goo is barely two centimetres deep, but it gushes stickily under your shoes as you walk. Ugh!

"Let's book," you say the moment you reach your friends.

Whew! Okay, you're still lost in the Danger Zone. But at least you're all together again.

Keeping an eye out for traps, the three of you go onwards. You're starting to wonder about this Danger Zone, though. "So what's so dangerous?" you ask Cammie and Jack.

Like an answer, a weird snuffling sound comes from the distance. You don't know what it is. And you don't *want* to know what makes it. You, Cammie and Jack start walking faster.

But the noise behind you comes closer and closer.

"Is it sniffing out our trail?" you ask worriedly.

Cammie peers over her shoulder. "It doesn't have to!"

Glancing back the way you came, you groan. Stretching behind you is a trail . . . of big gooey black footprints!

Thinking fast, you run to a doorway, leaving a clear trail. Then you kick off your shoes and toss them as far as you can!

"Quick. Go the other way!" you whisper.

Rush to PAGE 9!

22

"Okay, I'm ready," you declare.

Tex Loudsnore's test-tube crashes down. New puffs of smoke explode around you. You're surrounded by a rainbow-coloured cloud.

It feels as though a giant hand has landed on the top of your head. Down, down you go, pushed by this invisible hand. Your bones seem to grind together. Your muscles feel as if they're snapping.

Every nerve in your body is screaming in pain!

I never should have trusted Tex Loudsnore! *you think in horror.* He's just whipped up a potion to destroy me!

Is this the end? Find out on PAGE 98!

"What's the Danger Zone?" you ask. "And how could it be worse than a maze full of monsters?"

Jack only shakes his head. "No one knows," he replies. "Nobody's ever come out to tell us."

Yikes! You shiver. "So how do we get out?"

"I bet we aren't in it yet," Cammie argues. "After all, somebody marked this doorway with the sign." She taps the scratched D. "That must mean that it leads into the Danger Zone, and we should stay away."

Jack peeks round the doorway. "Hey!" he bursts out. "There's a mark on the other side of the door too. That means that *this* side leads to the Danger Zone too."

Jack and Cammie begin to argue again.

Sighing, you lean back against the plywood wall to rest your feet.

But when your shoulders hit the wood, the panel suddenly gives under your weight! It twirls round like a revolving door and dumps you on the other side!

Spin over to PAGE 87.

You trust Russell. After all, he's the leader. Alicia and Dan agree. The group starts to circle around. But after the first set of zigzags, Russell stops. "Spiders' webs," he whispers.

What's the big deal? you wonder. Spiders aren't so scary, compared to the maze monsters.

You peek around the corner — and gasp. The whole hallway is blocked by a giant spider's web! Sitting in the middle, its eyes gleaming, is a spider the size of an Alsatian.

The group sneaks away and tries another path. You walk and turn, turn and walk. . .

At last you come to a room that's different from the rest. The far wall isn't plywood — it's brick!

Russell climbs on Bob's shoulders. He prises out a few of the bricks. Hey, there's a hole in the wall. A tunnel!

High above, you see a gleam of bright sunlight.

Everyone turns to you. "It's up to you," Russell tells you solemnly. "You're the only one who can save us."

Turn to PAGE 78.

You float in the air in front of the metal monster's face. It sort of looks like Wally, except for the size — and the flashing glass eyes, the metal scales and the giant teeth.

And, it certainly *sounds* like Wally — only louder.

"I can't believe that the first time you switch, you become a hotshot superhero," he whines.

"Guess I'm just lucky," you reply. "But you shouldn't feel too bad. Being a monster is better than being a stupid sidekick."

"True," Wally agrees. "It *is* cool being a giant monster." A huge hand flashes forward to pluck you out of the air. "Because this monster gets to do you in."

"Funny, Wally." You laugh. "Remember, I'm Super-Doer."

You flex your supermuscles to get free.

Nothing happens. You're still trapped in the Wally-monster's gigantic hand!

Yikes! Turn to PAGE 46!

You glance round the building site. There's a pile of bricks, there's a cement mixer — and there's a bunch of those steel rods they use to strengthen concrete! Exactly what you were looking for!

You pick up a heavy bar, flex your mighty muscles. . .

Yes! The steel bends like thin wire.

"Hey!" a voice yells.

You glance up. A guy in a hard hat is glaring at you. "We were going to use that bar," he complains. "Now you've ruined it!"

You try to straighten it out. But you can't fix that last kink. Then an idea comes to you.

"I'll just heat this up with my magma-vision," you announce. You stare at the bent bar cross-eyed, the way Super-Doer does in the comics. Sure enough, the metal gets hot — too hot! The middle of the bar melts away!

Whoops! Guess you need to practise with your cool new powers.

The workman looks pretty angry. But then he's distracted by a sudden burst of crashes and screams. Another guy in a hard hat dashes up. "Super-Doer!" he cries. "Some horrible creature is trying to knock down our building!"

Leap into action on PAGE 59.

Bob jumps again, and you help him over.

"Get down!" he whispers.

But at that moment, the beast arrives. You freeze in terror.

Now you know what was making that weird rustling noise.

The creature has the body of a giant snake. But its head is human.

Sort of.

In place of hair, hundreds of tiny snakes wriggle on its scalp!

A hand grabs your ankle and yanks you down. Bob drags you along in silence through several corridors. Then he finally speaks up. "Pretty awful, huh? That's probably the most dangerous monster in the maze. It wraps around you, crushing every bone in your body. Then it swallows you. Whole!"

Turn to PAGE 6.

"I don't want to get this black gunk on my shoes," you declare. "Hold on a minute."

You creep along the edge of the big, black puddle. Your back is right against the splintery wooden wall.

About halfway round the puddle, you notice bubbles rising from the gluey goo. As they pop, they let out a horrible stink.

P-U! You squinch up your eyes and hold your nose.

Bad move! You should have kept an eye on the puddle. When you look again, a large, scaly head is rising from the glop.

That puddle must be a lot deeper than you thought!

A pale green forked tongue flicks out and wraps around your ankle. You can't pull loose!

Desperately, you claw at the plywood wall. But there's nothing to hold on to. And Cammie and Jack are too far away to help. You're dragged into the oily black goo.

You've got a sinking feeling. As your head goes under the surface, you realize: you're licked!

THE END

You gulp. Now you wish you hadn't been so eager to volunteer. But it's too late to back out. Bob appears with two more bigger kids — Dan and Alicia. "Let's go!" he exclaims.

The five of you set off. They keep you in the middle. You feel happy about that. Then you realize your "new friends" have a reason for keeping you safe. You're the only one who'll fit through Russell's way out.

You wind through the maze. Bob leads, his catapult ready. Everybody glances nervously around.

Then you hear a loud squishing sound.

"Oh, no!" Russell cries. "It's found us!"

Around the corner comes another horrible creature. This one has the body of a slug and a head like a giant squid!

Alicia grabs you as the thing rears up — and spits!

Turn to PAGE 18.

30

"Doc! You've got to listen to me!" you croak. "I'm not who you think I am! I'm not Ballistic Bug!"

"Sure," Dr Doof sneers. "You're actually the Queen of the May — and I'm the King of Albania!"

"Listen, you idiot!" you rasp. "I'm — urk!"

The armoured gloves tighten on your throat. Too late, you realize this wasn't the time to go insulting Dr Doof.

Frantically, you wave your hands, trying to get him to let go. Instead, the pressure just increases.

There's no talking to him. You'll have to use the magic words and find another, friendlier, mad scientist.

Your lips form the words, "Guest shot!" But you never speak them. Neither words — nor air — can get out of you.

No air can get in, either! Your lungs ache. Spots dance before your eyes. You're losing consciousness, fast.

Well, at least, you've learned one lesson.

Mad scientists get mad very, very easily!

THE END

You flutter your wings and arrow up into the darkness.

"Wait! Where are you going?" Dr Doof cries.

"I'm going to see if I can get away!" you answer.

You fly higher. You still don't see anyone.

"Hey! Hey!" you yell. "If there's anyone up there, listen! I'm not really Ballistic Bug. I'm just a kid! A kid who got trapped in a magic comic shop!"

You're gasping from the effort of flying so high and so fast. White spots form before your eyes.

Wait a minute — they're not spots. They're *stars*!

You're out of time, out of air . . . and out of luck. You're already plummeting back to Earth as you black out.

Next month, the new issue of Ballistic Bug is due to hit the stands. But when Horace Grumbacher arrives at his favourite comic shop to buy the new comic, it isn't there!

"Ballistic Bug has gone out of print," the shop owner explains. "But listen, kid. I've got a great new comic for you. The superhero is called the Powerful Pancake!"

He holds up a copy of a comic book with a squashed-looking superhero on the front. A superhero who looks a lot like you. . .

Too bad. What a flat ending to your story!

THE END

"O-okay, I give in," you croak. "You're scary."

The mutated Milo-monster grabs you with huge purple hands. Stinking slime oozes over you as he holds you in front of his face. His yellow eyes blaze.

"You're sure?" he demands. "You're sure I'm scary?"

You can't answer, because you're holding your breath. Boy, does he *reek*! The sour stench washes over you. You can feel it on your face. It stings. Like acid.

Milo shakes you. "Answer me!" his monster voice booms.

"Yes!" you scream. "Yes, I'm sure you're scary!"

Now it's not only your face that hurts. The skin all over your body seems to bubble and sag. So do the organs inside. Even your bones seem to be melting.

"What — what's happening to me?" you scream.

Your throat feels clogged with slime, and your eyes go all blurry. . .

Will you be able to read what happens on PAGE 113?

The crowd still isn't moving, and the robot is only a couple of giant steps away.

"Have you used these magic words?" you ask.

Wally nods. "I started out in another comic. I was some superhero's dopey sidekick. Then I met Alex, and we came here. All you have to do is think of another comic, and say the magic words."

"Okay. That gets you to another comic. But isn't there a way to get back home? Back to the real universe?" you ask.

Wally glances at you. "I think so. A mad scientist can send you. But you have to talk him into helping you."

You can barely hear him. People are screaming and bumping into you. "What're the magic words?" you beg.

Wally closes his eyes, thinking. Then he yells, "Guest shot!"

And he disappears!

You think of the two comics you'd been studying on the comic rack. Both of them have mad-scientist villains. Will the magic words take you to them?

Time to find out! You close your eyes.

To visit the world of Super-Doer, go to PAGE 104.

If you like Ballistic Bug better, turn to PAGE 66.

Tex Loudsnore cackles with glee. “How do you like my new batch of creature creator, Super-Doer? It even works on you!”

He grins evilly up at you. “I believe you’re my finest creation. You’re the biggest and scariest of them all.”

You take one angry, giant step towards Loudsnore.

The mad scientist yells, “Freeze, ugly!”

Your muscles suddenly lock up. You can’t move at all. In fact, you nearly fall on your horrible, tusked face!

Tex Loudsnore puts his hands in his pockets and beams up at you. “Best of all, my formula makes you my absolute slave. Now, you just stand there. Don’t move a muscle until I decide what to do with you.”

You try desperately to move — but you can’t!

Uh-oh! Can you move on to PAGE 67?

You recognize the other hero. It's Stinky Stanley, the mutant whose horrible breath is his weapon.

"The professor is waiting," Stinky Stanley calls.

Professor Yves Yaboum is also known as Professor Y. He's a powerful mutant, the leader of Y's Guys . . . and a famous scientist.

You follow Stinky Stanley to join the rest of Y's Guys. Then a flying chair enters the room. Seated in it is Professor Y!

He's hard to miss — after all, he's covered completely in bright red hair. In fact, he looks like an ape, except for those serious, wise eyes.

"Y's Guys!" he exclaims in a deep voice. "My mental powers have detected a disturbance in the great flow of being. Somehow, aliens from beyond this universe have invaded."

You gulp. Could Professor Y be talking about you?

You hope not. Especially when you hear what else he's got to say.

"We must destroy these invaders immediately!"

To ask Professor Y more about these aliens, turn to PAGE 17.

To try to talk the professor out of his planned battle, turn to PAGE 63.

You'll have to be fast — very fast — to veer away from the building. And there are other buildings all around you. You'll have to avoid them too!

There's only one direction to go. Tilting your body so it faces straight up, you pour on the speed.

Up, up you go. Faster. Faster. Now your body is a mere streak. You zoom past the building. Whoa. You're really moving!

In fact, you're moving so fast, you can't slow down. The air is getting thin. The sky darkens until you're in the blackness of outer space. There's no air at all out here. But that's all right. Super-Doer can hold his superbreath.

A second later, you notice something large and grey in your path. Oh, no! It's the moon!

Your superskin and maximuscles might have survived a crash into a house. But the moon is a different story.

"Aaaaaaaah!" you scream.

Nobody hears you in outer space. The air simply gets sucked out of your lungs. You don't even have the breath to yell, "Guest shot!" before you splat into the moon.

THE END

"I'll stick with a power I've used already," you decide.

You stare slightly cross-eyed at the big vault door, the way Super-Doer looks when he uses his magma-vision.

Nothing happens.

You try again. And again. You stare so hard, your head begins to pound. You're getting angry. All you see is red.

But you *smell* something odd — scorching paper.

You remember the time you burned a hole through a comic book by focusing sunlight through a magnifying glass. The paper turned brown, then it burned.

Suddenly, you notice that the flat, brightly coloured world around you is changing colour. Everything is getting brown. The sharp, burning smell is growing stronger.

Finally it hits you. You're *in* a comic book now! And somehow, your magma-vision has set the paper on fire!

You suck in breath to yell, "Guest shot."

But when you inhale, the smoke sends you into a coughing fit. You can't get the words out!

Flames crackle. Your body may be super, but it's only as strong as the paper it's printed on.

Is it getting hot in here, or is it you?

Actually, it's

THE END!

"What script?" you sputter.

"Oh, ha-ha, very funny," Dr Doof snaps. He shifts his grip on your throat. "The script says you're supposed to beat me by shaking the floor to pieces with your Super-Sonic Buzz-a-ronic power. But, no, you have to make a grandstand play with your little lightning bolt! Thanks a lot! I could have been hurt!"

Well . . . wasn't that the idea?

You blink in confusion behind your helmet-mask. This is too weird. Is Dr Doof saying that all those great comic battles — the ones you've always loved — are rigged?

Oh, well. At least that explains how the superheroes always win.

But you can't think about that right now. A furious Dr Doof is hissing in your ear, "Well? I want some answers, bug!"

You gurgle as his steel fingers tighten round your throat!

Take a deep breath and apologize on PAGE 83.

Bob moves confidently through the maze. In some areas, though, he motions for you to be quiet. You tiptoe along. And you notice that he keeps his catapult ready.

"This maze is an abandoned sub-basement for the whole block," Bob explains. "It's full of crazy, mixed-up animals. Each has its own hunting ground."

"And you fight them with that?" You point to Bob's catapult.

Bob shrugs. "It's all we've got," he admits. "I was lucky with the lion-thing. It just *hates* getting hit on the nose!"

Soon after, a weird noise echoes through the maze. *SHHHHH! SHHHH!*

Bob stops. His face turns pale.

"What —" you begin.

He shakes his hand at you. "Quiet!" he whispers.

Bob seems to be listening carefully. You realize he's trying to figure out where the sound is coming from.

At last he makes up his mind. "It'll be here in a second," he whispers. "Come on."

He boosts you up to the top of the wall, then leaps himself.

And misses! He bangs against the plywood. Then you hear a loud hissing sound.

Go to PAGE 27.

"Why?" you ask. "Why did you do this to us?"

Milo looks at you in surprise. "You know, you're the only one who's ever asked. This is the deal, kid. I've got a shot at a comeback. One of the TV networks wants to make a show out of *The Cellar of Scary Stories.*"

He frowns. "But they're not sure my stuff is scary enough. So I got my old creature crew together and GLOMPFed a bunch of you kids to see if we've still got it. What do you think?"

You remember the slow-moving Frankenstein's monster, the snoozing mummy, the toothless werewolf. "To tell you the truth," you answer, "your creatures seem pretty . . . lame."

"Lame?" Milo growls. "*LAME?*"

Your prisoner flings you off.

Uh-oh.

"H-hey, guys?" you call to the other kids. "Uh — I could use a little help. . ."

Milo makes a magical gesture. All the other kids disappear! You're alone with Milo the Mutant!

"So." Milo glares at you. "The greatest monsters of all time aren't scary enough for you. You think you could do better?"

Answer Milo on PAGE 135.

You try to run, but the snake-thing moves fast.

Its scaly body catches you on the shins. You stumble and fall to the floor. Before you can get up, the thing twists around you.

You can't move an arm or a leg. Thick coils of muscle have you all tied up.

The snake-thing's human face stares into your eyes as its grip slowly tightens.

The creature's lips stretch in an evil smile.

"You're sssso ssssmall, I should let you grow a bit more," it hisses.

"Really?" you squeak.

The snake's smile grows bigger and wider until its mouth is large enough to swallow you whole.

"Naaaah," the snake replies. "Just kidding!"

GULP!

THE END

42

Dr Doof wants to conquer your world? You never thought of that possibility when you asked for his help.

You've got to stop him! But how?

Then you notice something. Even though you're halfway into your own universe, you've still got the costume and the wings of Ballistic Bug. You can stop Dr Doof just the way the hero does in the comics!

"Oh, no, you don't, Doof!" you cry. You try to leap forward and grab Dr Doof.

But you can't move.

The hole in the universe has shrunk — and you're stuck!

Dr Doof laughs. "Soon the hole will close completely. It's curtains for you, bug!" Then he strolls off to terrorize your home town.

"Doof! Come back!" you shout helplessly.

Well, at least your top half made it home safely. But the shrinking hole cuts off your rear

END.

Looks as if luck is against you! You fall far short of the boy's reaching hands.

Instead, you bang into the wall, then crash to the floor.

You lie there, frozen. The lion-bull-eagle beast clomps closer. It growls in triumph.

Then the beast leaps backwards suddenly, yelping in pain. It paws at its nose.

What happened? Well — maybe luck is with you after all!

You look up. The boy is still leaning over the wall. He holds a catapult in his hand.

"Try again!" he yells.

You scramble to your feet. The patchwork beast lets out a furious roar.

Zing! Something flies past your ear. The beast yelps again. Bull's-eye! Right in the snout!

You leap again. A hand catches your wrist and hauls you up.

But the lion-creature is right behind you!

Head on up to PAGE 129.

Milo's ears twitch. He begins to turn round.

He heard you!

"Everybody run!" you yell.

Jack and Cammie take off as if they're training for the Olympics. You try your best to keep up. You can't let them out of your sight, or you'll be totally lost.

Your lungs are burning by the time your new friends stop. "Where are we?" Jack asks.

Cammie stares. "What do you mean? I thought *you* were keeping track of our route!"

They begin to argue. Great! Now you're *all* lost!

Jack suddenly breaks off and stares at the wall. He points. "Look!"

Both Jack and Cammie turn pale.

You glance at the symbol scratched into the plywood beside the doorway. A capital "D".

"What does it mean?" you ask.

"'D' stands for danger," Cammie whispers. She looks scared. "It means we've reached the Danger Zone!"

Find out more on PAGE 23.

Kid? You peer down.

You're not Super-Doer any more. You're yourself!

Hey! This is the vacuum shop that was next to the comic shop! "I was trapped in the comic shop," you gasp, pointing.

"You couldn't have been," the old man declares. "That place has been closed for years."

Huh?

You describe the comic shop owner. The old man gives you an odd look. "That was Milo. He died three years ago."

Whoa . . . have you travelled in time?

You ask for today's date. It's the same day as when you left for school this morning!

You dash outside, heart pounding wildly. The shops all look the same — except one. The windows of the comic shop are boarded up. The nails on the plywood panels are all rusty. The shop has obviously been sealed up for years.

You head for home, totally creeped out.

Could it have been a dream? It seemed so real. . .

One thing is certain. You'll never take another walk through this neighbourhood. And you hope you'll never, ever find yourself in the comic shop of horrors again.

THE END

46

"Wally," you cry. "Why are you doing this? We're pals — well, maybe not pals. But we go to the same school!"

"I'm sorry," Wally replies. "But the monster formula also makes me Tex Loudsnore's slave. He told me to destroy Super-Doer."

Uh-oh. Things are desperate. You give the Wally-monster a blast of your magma-vision. His shoulder begins to melt.

"Ow! Owww!" he yells. "I can't take this! I'm getting out of here! Guest shot!"

But when he yells the magic words, Wally doesn't vanish. A ripple runs through his giant form. The fingers round you feel strangely rubbery. His face looks runny.

He's melting!

Then you realize: Wally's time has come. He's used the magic words once too often. He's turning into an inkblot!

You strain to break away. You can't get free!

Holding up your hands in front of your face, you see with horror that *you're* getting runny too.

Bummer!

Your Uncle Mel always called you a little squirt.

But now you've turned into a big drip.

THE END

"No problem," you tell yourself. "I'll memorize my route!"

To make it easier, you decide to make only right turns. That works for the first four choices you face. Then you find yourself in a room with only one doorway — on the left.

By the tenth choice, you're mumbling to yourself, trying to remember which way you went. This place is definitely a maze. And it's bigger than the basement of the small comic shop. You feel as if you've been walking for miles. How can that be?

The next room you find is stacked high with old copies of *The Cellar of Scary Stories.* They're all the same issue that Horace showed you a slide of. The guy with the face like a warty pumpkin is the series host. His name is Milo the Mutant.

Hey! Now you realize why the comic shop owner seemed familiar. He looks just like Milo the Mutant!

This is starting to get creepy.

Then you hear a noise echoing through the maze. A slow, scraping sound — like a foot dragging on concrete.

Someone — or some*thing* — is following you!

What should you do?

If you go back and see who's following you, turn to PAGE 89.

If you'd rather get out of there — fast! — turn to PAGE 50.

You spin out of control, thanks to that shot from Wally. Wind blasts past you, making your cape whip about until it wraps round your head. You're ready to barf from all the tumbling. And your cape is blinding you.

Wait a second! You're Super-Doer. And Super-Doer can see through things with his cosmic-ray vision!

You try that slightly squinty look that Super-Doer gets when he uses this power.

The good news is that you can now see where you're going.

The bad news is that you're about to crash into a building!

To use your flying powers to veer away, turn to PAGE 36.

If you'd rather rely on your superskin and maximuscles to get you through safely, turn to PAGE 94.

"I — I could use a rest," you gasp.

Dr Doof releases you. "ALL RIGHT!" he yells, glaring into the darkness overhead. "We're taking a break! Put in an ad or something. Ballistic and I need to talk."

You stare upwards. Who's he talking to up there?

When you ask, the mad scientist shrugs in his armour. "Whoever runs this crazy world must be up there. That's where our scripts come from, anyway."

A brilliant idea bursts in your brain. Maybe you don't need the help of a mad scientist to get home. Maybe you can take your problem right to the person — or people — in charge of the Comic Books Universe!

If you stick with Dr Doof, turn to PAGE 95.

If you'd rather go over his head, turn to PAGE 31.

You walk faster and faster, until you break into a run. At first, the footsteps fade. Then you hear loud clomping. It sounds as if there's a herd of elephants hot on your heels!

You glance back as you go through a doorway. "Ow!" you yell. You brushed against jagged plywood. A six-centimetre splinter stabbed you in the arm!

Gritting your teeth, you pull the splinter out. Blood stains your T-shirt. From several turns behind you comes a rumbling roar. Uh-oh. Can whatever is chasing you smell blood?

The clomping sound turns into a crashing gallop.

You try to run faster. Flinging yourself through another doorway, you find yourself in a long hall. You're running flat out. But the stomping feet are right behind you.

One look over your shoulder — and you scream.

The creature chasing you looks as if it has been sewn together from several different animals. It has the body of a shaggy bull and huge, feathered eagle wings.

Worst of all, it has the head — and fangs — of a lion!

Run for your life to PAGE 54!

You head down the stairs. But after your first step, the whole stairway begins to shake. It's as if heavy machinery is working underneath.

The stair treads under your feet suddenly tilt. They crash down with an echoing mechanical sound. GLOMPF!

Now you know!

The stairway has turned itself into a slide! Your feet skid out from under you, and you bang your elbow. You're going faster, and you can't stop! You claw frantically at the slide. But you can't get a grip on the smooth metal. You don't even slow down — you just make a noise like nails on a blackboard.

It makes a good blend with your screams as you zoom faster and faster, deeper into the dark. . .

Speed on to PAGE 127.

Even if you climbed on each other's shoulders, you wouldn't make it up to the ceiling. But then you get an idea. . .

"Follow me!" you cry. Rushing to the storeroom, you pull on a box of comics. "We can use these to build a stairway!"

Jack and Cammie leap into action. You shift box after box, banging and crashing. These things are *heavy*!

"What's that noise? What are you doing?" Milo yells from his mirror. "Am I going to have to come down there?"

You're too busy to answer. You pile up a stairway of boxes. Jack and Cammie hold it steady as you scramble up.

The pile begins to shudder. As the cartons fall apart, you leap, clinging to the edge of the trapdoor. It takes all your strength, but you pull yourself through. You made it!

"I'll get help!" you call down to Cammie and Jack.

You peer around. You're behind the counter in the comic shop! The whole building shakes as boxes crash below. Comics flutter up through the hole. You grab one in mid-air and shove it in your pocket as you run for the door.

Below, Milo screams wildly. "You can't get away!" he howls. "You'll ruin everything!"

Hurry to PAGE 7.

Static electricity crackles around you. Lightning bolts zap from your head to blast the deadly hair balls in mid-air.

"Good shooting, RAY-ge!" Jean Greene shouts.

The other Y's Guys mob the professor. When the smoke clears, all that's left of him is a scorched spot on the rug. His mental powers were right. He *was* in deadly danger!

You turn to Wolfen-Bean. "How — ?" you begin.

The bean-warrior shrugs. "A couple of months ago, I walked into this weird comic shop and reached for this rack. . ." Wolfen-Bean grins. "It's cool. I *like* being a superhero!"

"But what about the danger?" you ask. "You could turn into an inkblot!"

"What are you talking about?" Wolfen-Bean demands.

You explain.

"No way," Wolfen-Bean scoffs. "We've got it made! Watch. Guest shot!"

"Stop!" you shout.

Too late. The bean-man's body shudders. He's melting!

The rest of Y's Guys glare at you.

"YOU!" Stinky Stanley shouts. "This is all your fault!"

Defend yourself on PAGE 132.

Hot breath ruffles your hair. The lion's roar deafens you.

When your ears stop ringing, you hear a voice yell, "Up here!"

You peer up to find a kid leaning over the plywood wall above you. He stretches out his arms to you.

"Jump!" he yells. "I'll pull you over!"

You don't need another invitation. You leap as high as you can, reaching for the boy's hands.

Will you make it? Is luck on your side?

Take a look at the hour hand on the clock.

If it's close to an odd-numbered hour — one, three, five, seven, nine or eleven o'clock — turn to PAGE 43.

If it's near an even-numbered hour — two, four, six, eight, ten or twelve o'clock — turn to PAGE 80.

This is kind of fun, you think. At last you're getting the hang of this superhero thing!

You buzz around the room, throwing punches at the air. You want to be ready for Dr Doof's next attack.

Then you notice that the evil doctor isn't getting up. He lies sprawled on the stage, helpless. Not moving.

Hmm. That shock shouldn't have knocked *all* the fight out of him, you think. In fact, his superarmour should have protected him against your Insecto-Electric Hornet's Sting.

Apparently it didn't work this time.

You start to get nervous. "Uh — Doc?" you call. You hover over the doctor's flat form. Is he still breathing?

Doof's metal-muscled hand moves like a striking snake. Before you can buzz off, he grabs you by the throat!

If you try to break free, turn to PAGE 119.

If you try to reason with Dr Doof, turn to PAGE 30.

You fire your Insecto-Electric Hornet's Sting at Dr Doof from across the room.

And miss! Your shot smacks into a blast-bolt Dr Doof had aimed at you.

The two bolts of energy explode together, throwing off rainbow-coloured sheets of flame. But in the middle of the fireworks display, there's a gaping black hole.

"Behold!" Dr Doof cries in a loud, hammy voice. "Our battle has sheared the very fabric of the universe. This hole could be a Doorway to Anywhere!"

Anywhere? you think.

Could it be a way out of this crazy Comic Books Universe?

You buzz forward, ready to zip through. Then you think again.

Doorway to Anywhere? That sounds kind of risky.

Maybe you should let Dr Doof go first.

If you go through the Doorway to Anywhere, turn to PAGE 19.

If you let Dr Doof test it first, turn to PAGE 100.

You eye the Wally-monster suspiciously. "Why didn't you ask Tex Loudsnore to get us out of the Comic Books Universe?" you demand.

"I didn't get a chance," Wally replies, sulking. "The second I entered his lab, he got me with creature creator juice."

Sounds likely. "Go and turn yourself in to the police," you order. "I'll deal with Tex Loudsnore!"

Leaping high into the sky, you head for Mount Skull. In the comic, Super-Doer never managed to find out where his arch-enemy's hideout was. But, since you've *read* the comics, you know exactly how to get there.

Minutes after leaving Bigg City, you spot a mountain shaped like a skull. You fly into the giant skull's left eye. It's a cave that leads deep into the mountain.

Six metres inside, your path is blocked by a steel door. With your Super-Doer powers, you know you can get through the steel door and talk with Tex Loudsnore.

The question is, which power should you use?

If you try your magma-vision again, go to PAGE 37.

If you test your strong breath, turn to PAGE 68.

You stumble out of the cave and into the bright sunlight of this comic-book world.

A tiny dot comes zooming down out of the sky.

What now? you wonder miserably. A missile? A meteor?

No, worse. It's Gnatman, Super-Doer's superhero buddy!

"Hold it right there, monster!" a whiny voice roars out from the hero's mouth.

Could it possibly be?

"Wally!" you yell. "You've got to help me!"

But once again, your words come out as a rush of flames. Gnatman flutters his gnat wings and zips out of the way.

"Oh, you want to play rough, huh?" Wally's voice sounds just like a gnat's annoying buzz.

But then he starts flitting around you, raining blows at super insect speed. *WHAP! KAPOW! BLAM!*

It's more than annoying. It's downright painful!

BAP! You crumple to the ground. Your giant body raises a huge cloud of dust. You start sneezing uncontrollably.

And that's just the beginning of your torture.

Oh, by the way — it's also the beginning of

THE END!

For a second you wonder what you're supposed to do. Then you remember. You're a superhero! It's your duty to save the building.

You leap up — and suddenly you're flying! Wind ruffles your hair. Your cape flaps behind you as you soar high over the building. You look down . . . and your jaw drops.

Just flying is incredible enough. But you didn't expect this!

Something the size and shape of a *Tyrannosaurus rex* is smashing at the building with its hands and tail. But the thing's scaly skin is made of shining metal. And your cosmic-ray vision shows that there's machinery inside.

The creature turns its glowing glass eyes on you. You expect an attack.

Instead, the robot dinosaur says in a whiny voice, "Oh, great! Now I've got Super-Doer after me."

You skid to a stop in mid-air. You know that voice.

"Wally?" you cry in disbelief.

If you try to talk things out with Wally, go to PAGE 25.

If you'd rather fight him, go to PAGE 102.

You leap straight into the air and zoom past Cammie and Jack. For the next few twists and turns through the maze, you lead the way. They finally catch up with you.

"Take it easy," Jack pants. "Old Menes probably went right back to sleep."

"Yeah," Cammie adds. "After a couple of thousand years, he needs his rest."

"That — that —" you gasp. "That really was a mummy?"

Cammie nods. "The maze is full of old-time monsters. That's why you have to —"

"Look out!" Jack suddenly yells.

You turn, just in time to see a figure leap from the top of the maze wall. All you see is a pair of blazing red eyes, flying towards you.

There's barely time to raise an arm to protect yourself. The eyes are right on you. You feel hot breath on your face. . .

Then jaws clamp shut on your arm!

Use your free hand to turn to PAGE 101.

But what comic will you jump to?

One of your favourites is *Silent Sal,* the comic book about teenagers. But there are no mad scientists there. Well, you could try *Super-Doer*.

But you'd better make up your mind fast. Ballistic Bug is zooming straight at you.

He's going to flatten you!

Hey! You've got it. There's another comic book that you like. It's about a supergroup of mutants, Y's Guys. Their leader is a super-scientist! That's the same thing as a mad scientist, right?

Ballistic Bug's fist is about thirty centimetres from your nose.

Keeping the Y's Guys in mind, you yell, "Guest shot!"

Just before his fist connects with your jaw, Ballistic Bug fades out.

Whew!

You start to fade in on another scene. But before you can make out any details —

"Look out!" a voice yells.

Fade in fully on PAGE 74.

Pretending you're still frozen, you watch Loudsnore work at his computer. The huge, complex machine even speaks!

"New data entered from manipulation of transuniversal phlogiston," the computer reports.

Huh? Oh, well. Just because the computer can speak doesn't mean you can understand it.

The mad scientist turns to you. "I've decided what to do with you," he announces. "I've sent for another of my creatures. I'm going to send you both to destroy Bigg City!"

You can't keep still any longer. This calls for action!

You wait until Loudsnore turns his back. Then you lean down and scoop him up. "In your dreams, Loudsnore," you growl.

"You can't do this!" Loudsnore sputters. "I control you!"

"Wrong," you reply. "Right now, I control *you*!"

Whoa! This is pretty excellent!

"First," you tell him, "I want you to change me back to Super-Doer." You figure it would be a good idea to have superpowers while dealing with Tex. "And next —"

But your next demand is drowned out. Thunderous footfalls echo through the cavern!

What now? Find out on PAGE 88.

"But, Professor, why?" you blurt.

"Yes?" the professor replies.

"No — I mean, Professor, why —"

"That's my name," Professor Y snaps. "Don't wear it out."

"I — I mean —" you stammer. You try again. "Why do you want to attack these visitors, professor?"

Professor Y's eyes gleam. "If you have to ask that, you're no true Y's Guy!" he declares. "You're an alien spy!"

His hair starts to grow, reaching out to you. You've seen pictures of this in the comics. But actually seeing the hair creeping around is, well, creepy.

Whoops! You spent too much time staring. When you tear your gaze away, you notice that tentacles of hair have wound around your ankles. You can't pull free!

There's only one thing you can do now. It's risky. But you've got to use the magic words.

"Guest — mmmmmph!" Your cry is muffled as still more hair attacks you, stuffing your mouth.

There's no escape now. Your doom is too horrible to describe. How horrible?

Let's just say that from here on, it gets really hairy. . .

THE END

"Why should I trust you, Loudsnore?" you demand. "How do I know what's in that test-tube?"

"I've got a Super-Doer robot you can test it on," Tex Loudsnore suggests.

You shrug. Sounds reasonable. "Where is it?" you ask.

"I keep it in that special box over there." Loudsnore points to a man-sized metal container by his lab table.

The box has no seams. There's no lid, no way to open it. So you crack it in two. Out pops a six-foot chunk of glowing, orangey-grey rock.

It lands on your foot — and sinks in!

Tex Loudsnore cackles. "That's Ziptite, the one substance in the universe that can kill you, Super-Doer! In case you're wondering, it *will* do the job, even though you're a giant lizard with tusks."

You hardly hear. Searing pain shoots up your leg and through your body. Black spots appear before your eyes. And grow.

The poison rock is all through you now. You're done for. You topple to the ground.

Your one consolation is that you land on Loudsnore!

THE END

Your heart is pounding so hard, you can barely hear anything. But you strain your ears as you tiptoe down the shadowy corridors. You peek carefully round every corner.

You can't hear Frankenstein's monster's shuffling footsteps any more. Even his roars of "NYAARRGH!" have faded away.

You've lost him!

With a sigh of relief, you lean against a plywood wall. A moth flutters past you. And a hand grabs it in mid-air.

Hey! That's not *your* hand!

You spin round to face two kids about your own age — a red-haired girl and a boy with shaggy dark hair. He's chewing on something. Both give you odd, close-mouthed smiles.

"I'm Cammie, and this is Jack," the girl tells you. "I guess you got GLOMPFed, just like we did."

"How long have you guys been here?" you ask.

"We're not sure." Jack swallows noisily. "But I know I had short hair when I got here."

You look at Jack's wild mane. This is bad news.

Go to PAGE 117.

You shriek at the top of your lungs: "Guest shot!"

When you open your eyes, everything is still dark. For a second, you think it's the shadow of the robot's foot coming down. Then you realize: it's night-time!

With a sigh, you lean against a nearby brick wall. You made it! You're safe! Of course, now you have to find out where you are. Too bad it's so dark. . .

Suddenly, yellow light glares around you. You blink. You're blinded! Then you hear a faint buzz. It rises to a whine. Your dazzled eyes see a figure in a tight brown costume with flashing insect wings coming out of its back.

Ballistic Bug!

"You're in big trouble," the bug says menacingly.

Trouble? You look down. There are tools in your hand. You also notice an open safe next to you.

Uh-oh.

You're a burglar. Ballistic Bug doesn't like burglars.

You'd better jump to somewhere new — and fast!

To jump to a different adventure of Ballistic Bug, turn to PAGE 70.

To try a totally new comic, turn to PAGE 61.

Whistling, Tex Loudsnore potters round the lab. He walks past you as if you were a huge statue.

You can't even move your mouth to say the magic words that would whisk you out of here.

Now he's working on some sort of formula. Smoke wafts up to the ceiling of the cave — right past your giant nose. The smell is nasty. You twitch your nostrils to keep from sneezing.

Wait a minute! Tex Loudsnore told you not to move a muscle, but you *moved*! Maybe the formula doesn't work as well as Tex thinks. Maybe this "absolute slave" thing is fading away!

You decide to test your theory. You try bending the little finger on your right hand. (Of course, now that "little finger" is over a metre long!)

The finger finally bends. Next you work on your hands and feet. Finally, you turn your head.

The mad scientist is still working. He hasn't noticed.

How are you going to use your freedom?

If you jump Tex Loudsnore, turn to PAGE 73.

If you keep still and spy on him, go to PAGE 62.

You suck in as much air as you can. Then you let it out with a WHOOSH! as if you were blowing out the candles on the biggest birthday cake in the world.

The door flies off its hinges and lands with a crash in the long hallway beyond.

As you walk down the corridor, you find that Tex Loudsnore has other defences. All sorts of weapons attack you.

But you're Super-Doer! Deadly poison gas only makes you sneeze. And Tex Loudsnore's disintegrator beam merely gives you a terrible itch!

"Wow!" you exclaim. "This is incredible!"

You could get used to being a comic-book hero.

The hallway ends at another steel door. No problem. Winding up, you smack it with your Power-Punch!

See what happens on PAGE 136.

"Yikes!" you shout. "Everybody *run*!"

You push. You shove. You try to get out of the giant robot's path. But the crowd is too thick. You're trapped.

"Hey!" a whining voice says in your ear. "I know you!"

You turn and spot a familiar face in the crowd. It's a kid from school called Wally. Come to think about it, he hasn't been in class lately.

"Where are we?" you cry. "What's going on?"

"You just got here on the spinner-rack express, huh?" Wally asks. "Okay, I'll make this fast. You're stuck inside a comic — in the Comic Books Universe."

You roll your eyes. "Yeah, right."

"It's true!" Wally insists. "Now here's the deal. We can shift from comic to comic, using a magic word. But if you use it too often, you'll turn into an inkblot." He shudders. "It happened to the kid I was with. Alex. He tried to leave this comic. Now he's just a smear."

You glance anxiously at the robot. It's awfully close.

"We'll be smeared too if we don't get out of here!" you declare.

Turn to PAGE 33.

You think hard. Then you yell, "Guest shot!"

Instantly, the shadows vanish in bright fluorescent light.

"Golly," a voice says in your ear. "Look at that!"

You look around. Huh? You're in the middle of a bunch of school kids dressed in old-fashioned clothes. What's the deal? You expected to find yourself in another adventure of Ballistic Bug. Instead, you've been dropped into some nerdy school trip.

Nervously, you glance upwards. With your luck, another giant robot will turn up any second.

"Gosh, Peewee," the girl beside you exclaims. "We're visiting a nuclear power plant! Isn't this neat?"

"Yeah," a bigger kid with a black crew cut sneers. "Maybe for a dweeb like Peewee Parkbench."

Is he talking about you?

You glance down at yourself. Your eyes bug out. Weirder and weirder! You've changed into a nerdy-looking character in a bow-tie.

Then you realize who you're supposed to be.

Peewee Parkbench, the secret identity of Ballistic Bug!

Turn to PAGE 72.

"Well," you reason, "if Frankenstein's monster catches up with me again, I can always run faster."

But the idea of Frankenstein's monster popping up again worries you. You turn to glance over your shoulder as you run.

BONK!

You see stars. You ran straight into a wall!

You glance quickly round the room.

Hmm.

There's no way out, except for the doorway you entered.

And standing in that doorway is. . .

Frankenstein's monster.

The creature doesn't even snarl as it stalks towards you. You're caught, fair and square.

And, as Frankenstein's monster starts painfully trying to unscrew your head from your neck, you remember how the monster caught its victims.

They all wound up running into a dead

END.

The kid with the crew cut pushes past, stomping on your toes.

"Hey!" you complain in a geeky voice. "Watch it!"

"Make me," Crew Cut sneers.

You grin. Okay, he asked for it.

You try to call upon Ballistic Bug's insect strength.

Nothing happens!

Then you remember what the girl next to you said. This must be the famous visit to the nuclear plant. The one where Peewee *gets* his incredible superpowers.

You don't have them . . . yet.

Get the details on PAGE 120.

It's a simple choice. Of course you jump Tex Loudsnore!

Not that it's easy. He runs around, yelling, "Halt! Stop! I command you!" And you have to be careful not to stomp him accidentally. He's your ticket out of this crazy comic-book world!

Finally, you catch him. Holding him carefully in one fist, you bring the mad scientist up to your face. "You're going to help me get home!" you demand.

At least, that's what you meant to say. But instead of words, flames come roaring out of your mouth.

In seconds, the only man who could have helped you is extra-crispy!

"Oh, no!" you gasp. More flames roar from your lips.

There's only one thing left to do.

"Guest shot!" you try to cry.

But since you can't speak, you don't vanish. Your despairing words once again lash out as flames, setting the laboratory on fire!

Go to PAGE 58.

You glance up. A huge hammer is hurtling towards your head!

You throw up your hands. But you know that won't stop the falling hammer. You're dead!

Your skin suddenly starts to tingle. Sparks fly around your hair. Then a lightning bolt flies from your head. It smashes the hammer to bits!

Your jaw drops. You stare at the pieces of wrecked hammer. "No way! This can't be happening!" you blurt out.

While you blink in disbelief, the wreckage fades away. You're in a bare, gleaming room with a grid on the walls.

You've seen this place before! It's the Peril Parlour, where Y's Guys practise their powers against holograms.

And that means. . .

You glance down at yourself. Sure enough, you're in the pink-and-blue uniform of Y's Guys. And with that lightning bolt on your chest, you'd have to be. . .

"Yo, RAY-ge," another pink-and-blue hero calls to you. "Professor Y wants to see us."

Professor Y! That's the scientist you want to see!

Meet the professor on PAGE 35.

The hazzafrazza device looks much safer! you think.

You stand under the floodlight on a set of copper and steel circles, one inside the other.

Tex Loudsnore starts pulling switches. The floodlight winks into life. Eerie, pulsing light shines down on you.

All of a sudden, you feel very strange. It's as if your body is stretching. Hey! This is sort of how you felt when the comics rack was spinning! Are you on your way home?

The lab fades away. But you can still see Tex Loudsnore dancing around, cackling.

"I'm your *worst enemy,* Super-Doofus!" he shouts. "Did you really think I was going to help you? The hazzafrazza device is a *matter transmitter.* And I set it for the centre of the star Vega!"

You try to scream, but no sound comes out. The lab has gone. A brilliant glow surrounds you. The glow gets brighter and brighter — not to mention hotter and hotter.

Too bad. But look on the bright side. At least you got to be a real star in

THE END!

"Hey!" you shout, flying straight at the shop owner's face. The closer you come, the bigger his face seems to get.

In fact, the closer you come, the bigger the *whole guy* looks.

Oh, no!

You escaped from the comic, but something went terribly wrong. You're still the size of a comic's drawing! You're barely five centimetres tall!

A shadow falls over you. It's the shop owner's hand, whipping down to swat you!

Maybe he thinks you're just another bug. Or maybe he knows exactly what you are, and he doesn't want you to escape.

Or maybe —

SPLAT!

THE END

You shake a fist under Milo's nose. "Okay, Milo, it's over!" you yell. "Let us all go — or you'll be sorry!"

Milo just laughs! "No, *you'll* be sorry! Don't you know I'm a mutant? I can change into any kind of creature I want to be." He gives you an evil smile. "Here's one I call — the Glob!"

The chest you're sitting on starts to wobble like jelly. You gasp as Milo's skin turns transparent.

Then he dribbles bonelessly out of his clothes!

Cammie and Jack leap back, screaming.

You try to jump too. But Milo's new form oozes around your legs. He's not just gooey, he's glue-y. You can't get free of Milo's slimy self!

He's up to your knees . . . your hips . . . now you're almost completely covered by the Glob.

Desperately, you try to peel Milo's glob-form off yourself. "HELP!" you try to shriek. But your air is cut off.

You look at your arm. Your flesh is beginning to blur.

Milo is absorbing you!

Too bad. You *looooze* this time!

THE END

Heart beating, you push past your friends — and into darkness. There's not much room. You're hemmed in tight. But you can see a light up ahead.

You pay attention to nothing else, working towards it. The light becomes dazzling. Blindly, you shove your way forward, feeling squashed and breathless.

You can't move! Are you trapped?

With a desperate wriggle, you force yourself a few centimetres forward.

Then, like a cork popping out of a bottle, you're through!

You tumble flat on your face. Rough concrete scratches against your cheek. You feel sun on your back. You're free!

Scrambling to your feet, you dash along a back alley and out into the street. "Help!" you yell. "Kidnapping! Monsters!"

Passers-by on the street turn round. You gape in horror.

These people have skin like dark green leather. They have giant, honeycombed eyes. Like insects. And they don't talk.

They *buzz*!

Buzz on to PAGE 16.

Russell almost bursts into applause when you catch your ankle. "You're just the person we need!" he cries. He turns to Bob. "Quick, get the others. We'll be leaving right away!"

Leaving? You were hoping you could stay at their camp. Somehow, it sounds safer than the rest of the maze.

And another thing. "*Why* am I just the person you need?" you ask suspiciously.

"Because of your size," Russell answers. "Everybody in our group is too big."

A shiver runs down your spine. "Too big for what?" you want to know.

Russell looks one way, then the other. He almost seems afraid he'll be overheard. "We think we've found a way out of here!" he whispers. "But it will only work for a little person!"

Turn to PAGE 5.

By sheer luck, you grab hold of the waiting hands. The boy pulls you out of the way — just in time. You look down at the lion-bull creature's furious eyes.

"Missed me!" you shout.

The creature roars as you swing down off the wall. A second later, the plywood wall seems to explode!

You duck as pieces of heavy wood framing fly past. What a mess! A pile of wreckage covers the lion-bull creature. It must have rammed down the wall and crashed into the next one!

"Help!" a voice cries.

You turn to your rescuer — to find him pinned under a pile of wreckage!

Pull him loose on PAGE 85.

There's something vibrating on your back. You crane to see over your shoulder.

Wow! You've got wings! Giant, shimmering insect wings!

You're so astonished, you freeze. That includes your wings, which stop beating. Instantly, you drop about a metre.

Lucky for you! A blast of energy sizzles right over your head. The blast-bolt! It explodes where you should have been.

Your wings start to buzz again. You notice now that your body is encased in some kind of sparkling brown armour.

Excellent! Your new "guest shot" has turned you into the star of the comic — Ballistic Bug!

You zip around, ducking Dr Doof's blast-bolts. Then you realize: you can fight back! You've got other superpowers besides your insect wings.

You'd like to try out your Insecto-Electric Hornet's Sting. But you're pretty far away from Dr Doof.

Should you try a blast from where you are? Or should you close in so your aim will be better?

Turn to PAGE 56 for long-range sharp-shooting.

Turn to PAGE 92 to make it up close and personal!

For the first time since touching that comic rack, you feel a little hope. "Could you really get me back home?"

Loudsnore rubs his chin. "Well, I need to run some tests, to see if your atomic composition is different from ours. And then there's the effect of the transuniversal phlogiston. . ."

You don't understand a word the mad scientist is saying. But you're eager to help. "Just tell me what to do," you cry.

Loudsnore points to a big metal box. "Climb in there."

In *there*? Maybe it's your imagination, but the box looks like a big coffin. Is Loudsnore *really* trying to help you? Or is he trying to destroy you?

"Isn't there some other way you could do these tests?" you ask nervously.

Loudsnore shrugs. "We could try the hazza-frazza device," he says. He points to something that looks like a huge floodlight, dangling from the ceiling. "But I won't get as good a reading."

Do you want to get into the coffin? Turn to PAGE 130.

Do you want to try the hazzafrazza device? Go to PAGE 75.

"Look, Doc," you croak. "I'm sorry, okay?" Then you get a bright idea. "I'm in so many different series — I, uh, get mixed up sometimes about which script is which."

Dr Doof scowls. "Sure, rub it in about how popular you are. I don't know what all those fans see in you, with those stupid antennae sticking out of your helmet. Anybody with any brains could see I've got a cooler costume!"

There's one good thing about this weird situation. Dr Doof seems like a reasonable man — sort of. Once he calms down, you should be able to talk to him!

Doof gives you one more shake, then sighs. "Well, we've got a job to do — unless you want to call a break."

To continue this phoney fight, turn to PAGE 126.

To take a break, go to PAGE 49.

Whoa! Milo must have read your mind. And changed himself into your worst nightmare!

His new body heaves and wobbles. He stares down at you through King Jellyjam's gooshy yellow eyes.

"Well?" he asks in a deep, gurgling voice. "What do you think? Am I scary enough?"

You gag. You'd almost forgotten that King Jellyjam had disgusting bad breath. But Milo got it down perfectly.

Your teeth are chattering so badly, you can't answer right away. But that gives you a chance to think.

Is Milo playing with you? Does he just want you to admit you're scared before he does you in?

On the other hand, Milo is in an unfamiliar body now. Maybe he doesn't know how it works yet. Maybe you should try to beat him!

If you admit that you're scared, turn to PAGE 32.

If you want to go up against Milo, turn to PAGE 14.

The good news is that the pile of stuff on top of your new friend isn't as large as the mound that buried the lion-bull creature.

You start tossing aside the pieces of wreckage. It isn't easy. The wooden beams that held up the walls are thicker than your arms. Big chunks of wood lie under smaller ones. You quickly learn this stuff can get heavy!

"What's your name?" you puff as you kick a three-metre beam off to one side.

"I'm Charlie," the trapped boy replies. "There's a bunch of us down here. If you meet my friends, tell them what happened to me. But get out of here," Charlie begs. "Save yourself while you can!"

"No!" you shout. "I'm going to help you, and that's final!"

Work your way to PAGE 121.

You laugh to yourself as you run through the maze. Frankenstein's monster may be strong, but he's so *slow*! How did he ever catch people in the movies?

The creature's cries get even fainter as you pound along. Finally, at the end of a long hall, you stop to catch your breath.

But you've only rested for a moment when a familiar shadow appears against the wall. A second later, Frankenstein's monster comes staggering down the hall. His clawlike hands grope for you.

"NYAAAAARRRRRRGH!" the creature cries.

The scent of decaying meat fills your nose.

He may be slow, but he's still plenty scary. Shuddering, you dodge through the first doorway you see. Dashing down a new hall, you quickly outrun the monster's staggering steps.

"Man!" you mutter. "That was too close! How did he catch up with me so quickly?"

Then you get it. Of course. The creature *lives in the maze*! It knows all the short cuts!

Run to PAGE 71.

You pound against the trick panel. It doesn't budge! "Jack! Cammie!" you yell. "What's going on?"

They shout back, "We've never seen a wall like that before."

In spite of everything you do, the wooden panel stays stuck.

"Just keep going," Cammie calls to you. "Sooner or later, the maze must come together again."

You go through the nearest door and into the hallway beyond, shouting to your friends. But after a few turns, their voices sound further away. And then you can't hear them at all.

Then you hit another big room. It's different from anything else you've seen in the maze. The floor is covered by a puddle, metres wide. There's just a little bit of dry space by the walls. "What is that stuff?" you mutter. It looks like black ink!

Hearing your name called, you look up. There's a doorway at the other side of the room. And there are Jack and Cammie!

"Come on!" Jack cries. "Let's get out of here!"

You could walk through the gloppy puddle. Or maybe you should try to edge round it, hugging the walls.

If you walk straight through, go to PAGE 21.
If you try going around, turn to PAGE 28.

The footsteps get louder. Louder.

And then one of Loudsnore's horrible creations stomps in. It's a dinosaur-like creature made of metal and plastic.

And it looks a lot like your friend Wally.

Loudsnore points at you. "Destroy this monster!" he orders the new creature. "But don't hurt me."

"Don't listen to him, Wally!" you shout. "He doesn't really control you."

"Huh?" Wally's glowing eyes look confused. "Hey! I'm not doing what he said. I guess he *doesn't* control me."

You grin. "So, where were we?" you ask Loudsnore. "Oh, yes. You were giving me back my Super-Doer body — and de-monsterfying my friend too."

Holding Loudsnore by the collar of his lab coat, you dangle him from your giant hand.

"All right!" screams Loudsnore, clinging desperately to your fingers. "I'll turn you both back!"

Now he's talking! Turn to PAGE 99.

"Okay," you tell yourself. "So I'm being followed through a dark maze. I should look on the bright side. Maybe whoever it is can show me the way out of here."

You turn back on your trail. As you do, you notice a nasty smell in the air. It reminds you of the time your uncle Mel left the bag of rubbish in the kitchen when the family went on a two-week holiday. And it seems to be getting stronger.

Uh-oh.

You pop round a corner and into a room. Light pours through a second doorway. It throws a moving shadow on the wall.

Maybe it's Milo, or whatever the owner's real name is.

Then the figure arrives in the doorway.

It's not Milo.

This guy is *tall.* And he doesn't have a face like a rotten pumpkin.

His skin is greenish-grey, like mouldy cheese. Puckered scars run up his cheeks. A pair of big, metal bolts stick out of his neck.

It's impossible — but he looks like Frankenstein's monster!

When he sees you, he snarls, "NYAARGH!"

Turn to PAGE 115.

"Doc? Hey, Doc? Are you okay?" you shout into the hole in space.

No answer.

Taking a deep breath, you stick your head through the hole.

You blink. You're gazing at an everyday street — outside a very familiar comic shop. Dr Doof is standing there, peering in the window.

"What were you screaming about?" you demand.

"This world is so different," Dr Doof replies. His voice shakes.

You realize he's used to the flat, bright universe of the comics. "Yeah," you reply. "I guess the colours seem pretty dull."

"It's a drab world," Dr Doof agrees. "But a whole new world for me to conquer!"

Uh-oh! Hurry to PAGE 42.

Dr Doof spins you over his head like a baseball batter doing warm-ups. "Whoa! Yow!" you screech as you fly around in circles.

"Oh, good. That's good," Doof compliments you.

"I'm not faking it!" you try to yell. But you're so dizzy, you can't get the words out.

Then Dr Doof hurls you away!

"Aiiiiieeeee!" you yell. You're hurtling straight at a brick wall. Head first!

"Tuck and roll, bug-brain!" Doof howls. "You'll break your neck!"

If you were a trained comic-book professional, you'd know what to do. But since you aren't, you don't . . . and this is

THE (*CRUNCH!*) END!

You dodge two more blasts from Dr Doof, then zoom into a dive-bombing attack.

Your Insecto-Electric Hornet's Sting is built into your helmet's antennae. The charge builds up all through your body. When you're almost on top of Dr Doof, you let it go.

FZZT! A bolt of green energy leaps out of the antennae. It slams into your enemy's chest, knocking him flat.

"Hah!" you cry. You do a triumphant loop-the-loop in the air. "Take that, Doof!"

Zoom to PAGE 55.

"Please," you beg. "I need help. My friends are trapped —"

Still shrieking, the bug-people start backing away.

"Noooo!" you shout. You run after them. But they jump like huge crickets — seven metres at a leap! In a couple of blocks, the bug-people leave you far behind.

But one of them can't jump away. He — or it — is trapped under an overturned cart. It looks like a rolling hot-dog stand, except the sausages are wriggling, wormlike things.

You lean over the trapped alien. "Listen to me —" you begin.

The bug-person flops back. It's fainted!

Clearly, you're not going to get any help here. You'll have to go back to the basement and rescue your friends yourself.

But — how do you get back? How can you find the alley where you arrived on this world? As you gaze around, you realize that all the buildings are identical. Hivelike.

It seems you're stuck on this strange world . . . a world where *you're* the monster.

Oh, well. Don't bug out!

THE END

Ker-WHAM! You hit the wall with a tremendous crash — and keep on going! At least your cape is off your head now.

Bang! Crash! You smash your way through other rooms in the building. But your superskin isn't even scratched. Amazing!

You thump through one more wall before you come to a stop. Time for a little payback! You rocket out through the series of holes you already made in the walls.

Quick as a flash, you zoom back to the Wally-monster. *POW! BOP! BIFF!* You unleash your Power-Punch on Wally.

"Hey! Ow! Not fair!" Wally whines. "It's not my fault. I didn't want to be a monster. Tex Loudsnore turned me into one!"

"Tex Loudsnore?" you repeat. Hmm. Not only is he the top villain in Super-Doer comics, he's also a mad scientist.

Just the guy you need!

Move on to PAGE 57.

You decide to try for Dr Doof's help. After all, he doesn't seem like a bad guy, once you get to know him.

"Look, Doc," you whisper. "I have a big problem. I don't really belong here."

You explain about the comic shop and what happened to you. Dr Doof listens without saying a word.

You wish he'd take off those goggles and the metal mask. It would be nice to see the expression on his face. What if he thinks you're just a total nutcase?

But you keep on, until you've told the whole story.

When you run out of words, Dr Doof stands there silently for a long moment.

"I always knew we were doing some sort of entertainment thing," he finally mutters. "But . . . comic books!" He shakes his head. "I'm so embarrassed."

Embarrassed?

"Forget about that," you reply impatiently. "Is there any way to get out of here?"

Dr Doof thinks it over.

At last, he declares, "Yes!"

Well, what are you waiting for? Go to PAGE 13!

"Um, wait a second!" you cry. "I'm not sure —"

But Tex Loudsnore has already started up the unconfrabulator.

Trying to duck, you cry, "Guest sh ——"

A spear of brilliant blue light leaps from the device. It catches you right in the chest. Oh, the pain! You scream.

Tex Loudsnore screams too. "I *told* you to keep still! Now you've ruined everything. You'll disintegrate. And *I'll* be stuck with Super-Doer again!"

You gaze down in horror as your body begins to crumple in on itself. You can't scream again, though. There's nothing left to scream with! You stretch out your hands and watch them grow fainter and fainter, until they've gone — and *you've* gone! You're nothing!

It's a shame. You always tried so hard to be cool.

But now you're a total zero!

THE END

The monster with Wally's face and voice reaches the top of the building. You get ready . . . and jump!

Whoops! You still need to get used to your new powers. You overshoot the building, speeding high into the sky!

Spinning in mid-air, you charge back. The Wally-monster has reached the top of the unfinished building. Your fist goes back for your Power-Punch. This time you won't miss!

As you zoom down, the Wally-monster grabs a big steel girder that sticks up from the top of the building. Tearing the girder loose, he slings it over his shoulder. Like a club. Or. . .

Whack! Too late, you realize Wally was holding the girder like a baseball bat. And he's using you as the ball!

You grunt as the steel beam strikes you. Even with your superskin and maximuscles, the impact knocks the wind out of you.

Wally's swing also knocks you out of the construction site. Tumbling helplessly, you streak towards the horizon like a line drive!

Swoosh to PAGE 48.

The colours fade away. Tex Loudsnore walks up and pinches you.

"Ouch!" you yell. That hurt! You wish you were at home in bed. You wish you were out of this comic.

Of course, you could yell, "Guest shot!"

But you don't want to risk turning into an inkblot. Besides, your only hope of escaping from the Comic Books Universe is to get help from a mad scientist. And here's one, right now.

"Ah-hahahahaha!" Loudsnore gloats. "I've done it! You've lost your powers!"

"I didn't want them," you reply. "Look, I'm not who you think I am. I'm really a kid in trouble. I need your help. . ."

As you explain how you wound up here, Tex Loudsnore's eyes narrow. "Incredible!" he exclaims. "Impossible!"

"That's what I thought, until it happened," you say.

"It sounds like an interdimensional hyper-flux," Loudsnore muses. "Very interesting. Let me see what I can do."

Hear more from the mad scientist on PAGE 82.

You put Tex Loudsnore down. He runs over to one of the lab tables. While he mixes chemicals, you keep an eagle eye on him.

Wally slides up to you. "Do you trust Loudsnore?" he whispers. "I mean, he's a villain — a bad guy!"

"He's also a mad scientist," you point out. "You said that's what we need to get home again."

"You trust him if you want to," Wally says. "I'm out of here." He takes a deep breath, then hollers, "Guest shot!"

But instead of disappearing, Wally clutches at his throat and screams! He falls back against the wall.

Then his body begins to melt all over the rock!

Horrified, you step towards Wally. He frantically waves you away. His screams turn to bubbling moans.

"The blot!" he coughs out. "I tried to jump once too often. I'm turning into an inkblot!"

It's too horrible. You squeeze your eyes shut.

When you open them again, all that's left of Wally is an enormous stain running down the wall and on to the floor!

Yuck! Go to PAGE 106.

100

You hang back. You want to know more about this Doorway to Anywhere before you try it out.

Dr Doof steps forward. "Fascinating!" he exclaims, leaning into the black opening.

Then, with a fearful cry, he's sucked in!

"Doc!" The cry bursts out of you.

Dr Doof clutches the edge of the black hole with one hand. He holds the other out to you. "Help me!" he shrieks.

You don't want to go near that hungry hole.

But you're supposed to be a hero, aren't you?

So you grab hold of Dr Doof's arm and pull. Your wings whine with the effort.

The mad scientist suddenly pops out. He sprawls on the floor.

The hole disappears with a sharp bang.

And Dr Doof grabs you by the throat, shouting, "Sucker!"

Gulp! Go to page 119.

"A werewolf!" you shriek. "Help! It's got me!"

Then you notice — your arm isn't bleeding. It doesn't even hurt.

The creature has no teeth!

Whining like an unhappy dog, the beast-man leaps away.

"You were lucky," Cammie says. "If that had turned out to be the Frenzied Flesh-eater. . ." She shakes her head.

"The maze creatures are all from Milo's horror comic," Jack explains. "Frankenstein's monster, Menes, Wolfie —"

"No way!" you burst out. "Those things don't exist!"

"You saw them," Jack insists. "It's Milo's magic."

Jack and Cammie start walking again. You tag after them. "Wait! If Milo is magic, why didn't he save his comic book? Why is he stuck running that dopey shop?" you demand.

You turn a corner and crash into your two guides. They're frozen in the doorway of a big room. It's full of kids — and facing them is. . .

"Milo the Mutant!" you gasp.

He hasn't spotted you. Should you jump him? Or should you run?

To tackle Milo, go to PAGE 123.

If you'd rather get out of there, run off to PAGE 44.

"School pal or not, you aren't wrecking this building!" you cry.

Flying down like an arrow, you aim for the Wally-monster's nose. You already have your fist stuck out to deliver your Power-Punch.

But when you arrive, Wally isn't there!

Desperately, you screech to a stop before you Power-Punch your way deep into the ground.

You whirl round to find the huge, prehistoric space-monster climbing up the building. Huge metal claws screech against the concrete walls as the Wally-monster pulls itself up. The noise is about ten times worse than the sound of fingernails on a blackboard. And since your super-ears are ten times keener than ordinary ears, it's downright painful.

"You'd better quit it, Wally," you warn. "You're beginning to annoy me!"

Keep up the fight on PAGE 97.

Your body feels as if giants have been using you for a game of tug of war. You're sick and dizzy from the spinning. But you notice something is wrong. The world seems strangely flat. The colours are very bright. You peer up at an incredibly blue sky.

Sky? Wait a minute! How did you get outside?

An elbow jabs you. Someone steps on your foot. You aren't just outside — you're in a crowd. And what a crowd! You're packed in so tightly, you can barely move. The person behind you is actually breathing down your neck.

Could this be a parade?

"What's going on?" you ask.

No one answers you. But a voice cries, "Here it comes!"

A shadow falls across you. When you see what's blocking the sunlight, your eyes grow big. It's a gigantic tin can — with arms, legs and a head. No — it's a robot!

"I don't believe this!" you gasp in a strangled voice.

You'd *better* believe it. That thing is as big as a skyscraper. And it's striding straight for you!

Go to PAGE 69.

"Guest shot!" you yell.

When you open your eyes, you're standing beside an office tower that's still being built. The crowd has gone. The robot has gone. You're all alone.

"This is bizarre," you mutter.

A voice suddenly yells, "Heads up!"

Of course, you look up. A falling brick hits you right between the eyes.

And bounces off!

You goggle in disbelief. That brick should have killed you. But it felt like a leaf being blown against you!

You look down at yourself. Hey! You've grown up. You have all kinds of muscles. And you're wearing what looks like purple long underwear with a big yellow "S-D" on the chest.

You not only switched comics, you turned into Super-Doer!

Cool!

"I've got to find a steel bar!" you exclaim. "Can I really bend it with my bare hands?"

Go looking on PAGE 26.

Using your superspeedy scramble, you rush forward to grab the flying test-tube. But this is another new power for you, and you don't quite get it right.

Tex Loudsnore's test-tube flashes past your fingers and shatters at your feet. Whatever is inside bubbles on the floor. Then you're surrounded by a cloud of red and green smoke.

"You'll need more than a smoke bomb —" you start to say.

But that's all you can choke out. Your eyes burn. Your lungs feel on fire. Even your skin hurts! It's stretched so tight, you're afraid you're going to burst like a balloon!

You're in pain. You're also confused. Nothing is supposed to be able to hurt you. You're Super-Doer!

Right?

Find out on PAGE 98.

Tex Loudsnore stares from you to the blot that Wally has become. "There must have been something wrong with that batch of creature creator," he declares. "I'd better run some tests on you. We don't want anything to go wrong when I change you back."

The mad scientist turns several weird instruments on you. He frowns. "My phenopticon is getting odd readings from you. My formula reacted very strangely with you."

"So?" you demand.

Loudsnore licks his lips nervously. "Well, I can give you back your Super-Doer body. But to do the job, I'll have to take your superpowers away!"

"Well —" you start to say.

"Trust me. I know what I'm doing," Loudsnore assures you. He starts mixing ingredients. In about a second and a half, he has another test-tube in his hand, ready to throw.

Wait a second, you think.

How do you know what he's got in there? How do you know he's not going to turn you into something even worse this time?

If you trust Loudsnore, turn to PAGE 22.

If you don't trust Loudsnore, turn to PAGE 64.

"We saw Milo last week," Cammie remarks. "The werewolf was chasing us. Milo popped around the corner and stared at us. Then he shook his head, like he was annoyed. 'I'll never make my comeback this way,' he said. Remember, Jack?"

Jack doesn't reply. He's staring over your shoulder. You turn to see a bug crawling up the plywood wall. A big bug.

Jack grabs for it. And Cammie *snarls* at him. It's a sound you'd expect from a wild dog, not from a kid. Jack and Cammie seem ready to fight. You notice how skinny they are. And dirty. And how long their fingernails have grown.

Suddenly, Cammie seems to remember you're there. "Look, you need help," she tells you. "Why not come with us?"

"Yeah, you can meet the other kids," Jack adds.

Your eyes widen. "You mean there are more of us down here?"

Jack nods. "We help each other."

Getting help, even from strangers, sounds good to you. But then again, you're not too far from that trick stairway. You might be able to find a way out on your own.

If you go with Jack and Cammie, move on to PAGE 124.

If you turn them down and go on alone, go to PAGE 112.

Everyone in the room is whooping and hollering to celebrate your victory. You peer down at the helpless former comic-book host. He seems oddly calm.

"Fine," you yell over the noise. "We've got him. Now what do we do with him?"

"Make him let us go!" one of the kids yells.

"Yeah," Cammie cries. "Milo must know the way out of here."

But you find yourself thinking back to the speech Milo was making when you tackled him. He said he had a very serious reason for keeping the kids in the maze.

What could it be?

If you tell Milo to let everyone go, turn to PAGE 77.

If you ask Milo what he's up to, turn to PAGE 40.

You gulp. But their faces seem friendly.

"Why don't you come with us?" Cammie suggests, stepping up to you. "You'll be just in time for dinner."

"That's right," Jack chimes in, taking your arm in a firm grip. You try to shake off his hand.

You can't get free.

"Uh — what is there to eat down here?" you ask.

"Oh, we just take whatever falls our way." Cammie grins at you. You suddenly notice how big her teeth are. How pointed.

Jack's smile reveals the same big, sharp fangs.

Hope you don't have a sweet tooth. Because it doesn't look as if you'll be around for dessert!

THE END

The trapdoor flies open more easily than you expected. You drop to your knees, eager to explore whatever is down there.

But there's no way down! No stairs. No ladder. Not even a rope to climb.

Fog seeps up through the open trapdoor. As the misty wisps touch you, you shiver. You've never felt anything so cold!

On instinct, you try to leap for the doorway. But it's already too late. Your muscles won't obey. They're frozen!

The fog is all around you now. A thin film of ice forms on your skin. Dimly, you notice Bob and another boy, peering through the doorway at you.

"You were right, Bob. It was a trap," the strange boy says. "That kid was just what we needed. Better a stranger should get hurt than one of us."

That's all you hear. Then the icicles on your front half pull you off balance. You topple forwards. Into the dark hole.

SPLOOSH! You plunge into icy black water. A swift current whirls you away. What's happening? you wonder foggily.

Then you pass out.

Wash up on PAGE 137.

Tiny grey dots swirl around you. They land, covering your arms, your hands, your face.

You try to brush the stuff away. It won't come off!

"Bugs!" Russell yells in horror. "They're teeny, tiny *bugs*!"

You feel a creepy-crawly sensation on your skin. Then it starts to sting — like millions of pinpricks. You blink your eyes and hold your nose, trying to keeps the bugs away. But you feel suddenly weak. It's as though these tiny things are sucking the juices right out of you!

Alicia keels over, hitting the floor. She's covered in grey gunk. She looks just like those piles of mould you passed in the other rooms.

You must look like one too, you think as you fall.

And soon, that's all you'll be. . .

THE END

You want to get out of this maze *now*. Besides, Cammie and Jack are too weird for you. "Thanks, but I'd like to see how I get along on my own," you tell them. You fake a smile. "Maybe I'll see you later."

You hurry out of the room.

Behind you, they start snarling at each other again. "You let that kid get away!" Jack's voice echoes through the maze.

"Oh, right," Cammie answers. "It was you and your bug-eating! You should *never* do that in front of newcomers."

"Speaking of bugs —" Jack's voice stops. But you hear a loud *crunch!* as if he's biting into something.

Something with a hard shell.

"Come on!" Cammie orders.

Then you hear their footsteps. Coming your way!

Do you run? If so, turn to PAGE 50.

Or should you try to hide? Turn to PAGE 125.

113

When your eyes clear, you find Milo standing over you. He's changed back to his usual ugly but not-so-scary self. A big grin stretches across his warty face.

"You d-didn't kill me?" you stammer.

Your voice! It comes out as a gurgling roar.

"Kill you?" Milo laughs. "Kid, you're my gold mine! I'm going to make you my partner — my star!"

"What?" You sit up — and bob squishily for a moment. What's going on? Why is Milo so far below?

You wipe a drop of sweat off your forehead. Eek! Where did that snail come from? And when did your hand turn purple?

Oh, no. Milo has mutated *you* into King Jellyjam!

"We'll make tonnes of money!" Milo gloats. He waves a hand in front of his face. "Of course, some of it will have to go on breath mints and deodorant for you."

Your show is a big hit. You start with TV, but soon you're starring in movies. Huge crowds turn out whenever you make a personal appearance. They love you!

But the real moneymaker is your El Grosso Snail Farms. Where do you get the snails?

No sweat!

THE END

114

You catch the test-tube, but the top pops off. Poof! The world disappears in a puff of purple smoke. Your skin begins to crawl. Your bones ache.

Then the cloud disappears. No — it's just down around your middle. The lab seems smaller.

No, wait. It's you. You're *growing*.

The purple cloud is further down, and the roof of the cave is coming closer and closer to your head.

That's thirty metres high! you think. That makes me —

Your thoughts get jumbled as your head bumps against the ceiling of the cave. You close your eyes, bracing yourself to get squashed against the roof. But it doesn't happen.

You've stopped growing!

Looking down at yourself, you realize you've changed. Your skin is green and scaly. And you have a thick tail.

Gulping, you run your fingers over your face. Oh, no! Bulging eyes, scales, sharp teeth, tusks —

Tusks?

What kind of monster has Tex Loudsnore turned you into?

Learn the worst on PAGE 34.

For a moment, you can't tear your eyes away from Frankenstein's monster. But when he lurches towards you, you leap away. You dash down a hallway. The creature's snarling cry echoes behind you.

As you race through the next doorway, you scrape against the rough plywood. Your jacket tugs you back when you take the next step. It's caught on a bunch of splinters!

You try to pull loose, but you can't get free! And here come the monster's scraping footsteps! Desperately, you wrestle out of the coat and keep running.

You turn left. Then right. Then right again. After a few moments, the creature's snarls become fainter. It sounds as if you're losing him!

Should you keep running? Or, now that he can't see you, should you try *sneaking* away from the creature?

One thing's for sure — you've got to find the way out of this maze. Fast!

If you run, turn to PAGE 86.
If you sneak away, turn to PAGE 65.

116

"Here, buggie-buggie," you whisper. You're worried. This is an important moment in comic-book history. If one detail isn't right, there might be no Ballistic Bug.

The glowing bug scuttles towards you. You stick out your arm. . .

Wow! Look at the size of that stinger!

The bug buzzes around your arm. Then it strikes!

"Yeeee-OW!" you yell. It's a lot more painful than Peewee Parkbench made it look in the comic.

In fact, it feels as if someone's injected molten lava into your veins. . .

You collapse, gasping. You can't feel your hands or feet any more. Something has definitely gone wrong.

Remember how you worried about one detail being different at this moment in history? Well, there was. *You* were here, not Peewee Parkbench.

And it seems you're allergic to mutant bug-bites.

Fatally allergic.

The world starts to vanish in a red haze.

Maybe you should start looking for a mad *doctor*. . .

THE END

"See, it's hard to guess time. We can't tell whether it's day or night in Milo's maze," Cammie explains.

"Milo's maze?" you repeat. "So the guy in the comic shop is called Milo? Like the guy from *The Cellar of Scary Stories*?"

"He *is* the guy from *The Cellar of Scary Stories*," Cammie replies. "Or he was. The comic was cancelled years ago."

"But if there's no more comics, how could — wait a minute!" you yell. "Comic characters aren't real! This is impossible!"

Jack just shivers. "With Milo, *anything* is possible. He blames kids for not buying enough of his comic books."

"Is that why he trapped us down here?" you ask.

Jack shakes his shaggy head. "We aren't sure. Sometimes we catch him spying on us. We think maybe he's trying to scare us."

"*Trying?*" you sputter. "I'm scared to death!"

Shudder along to PAGE 107.

"I'll go first," Cammie declares. She leans into the glowing mirror. Then she jumps back. "Whoa!"

A face has appeared in the mirror. Milo the Mutant!

"What are you doing in my room?" he yells.

"We've got to get away!" Cammie cries. She turns to you. "What was beyond your doorway?"

"Just a room," you reply, "full of boxes of comics."

"I didn't get a chance to look through my door," Jack complains. "You called me in here."

You hurry to Jack's doorway — and gasp. Stretching up to a trapdoor in the ceiling is a ladder. It's made of dark wood, carved into twisting shapes — snakes, dragons, weirder creatures. It's beautiful — but *strange.*

You step towards the ladder. It suddenly begins to glow red. Wind swirls round it, flinging you back. The glowing form shrinks down until it's barely twenty-five centimetres tall!

Milo's laughter echoes from the mirror next door. "That takes care of the magic ladder!" he cries. "Now I'll start the spell to take care of *you!*"

You gawk helplessly at the trapdoor in the ceiling. If only you could get up there. So near, and yet so far!

Move it to PAGE 52.

Your wings buzz frantically, but you can't break Dr Doof's choke-hold!

"Now I've got you, insect!" he roars, shaking you.

You try every trick you've ever read in a Ballistic Bug comic book. But nothing weakens the grip of those steel-clad fingers. You're about half a breath short of choking as Dr Doof climbs to his feet.

But then the evil doctor hauls you close and whispers, "Have you gone completely batty, bug? That sting-bolt of yours wasn't in the script!"

Script?

What's Dr Doof talking about? Find out on PAGE 38.

You tag along with the tour group, thinking hard. You don't even glance at the huge, powerful machines in the nuclear plant. Instead, you keep your eyes peeled for a glowing insect. That's the creature that will bite Peewee Parkbench and give him his amazing insect powers.

At last, you spot the bug.

Whoa, is that thing ugly! It's obviously some kind of nuclear mutant. It looks like an overgrown roach — with a huge, nasty stinger. You couldn't really see that part in the comics. All the picture showed was a line in the air and the word "BZZZZZ!" In the next picture, Peewee Parkbench yelled, "Ow!"

Now you can see why.

Do you really want to let that ugly thing sting you?

True, you want to make sure comics history doesn't change. But you also want to get back home. Maybe you should just jump to some other comic and keep searching for a mad scientist.

Better decide fast. The bug is coming your way!

If you use the magic words to leap to another Ballistic Bug adventure, turn to PAGE 15.

If you let the bad bug bite, turn to PAGE 116.

You roll, throw or shove battered pieces of wood away. Your arms are tired and burning from all this work. And you still face the hardest job of all. Charlie is pinned under a whole sheet of plywood. How are you going to lift a slab of wood twice as tall as you are — and three times as wide?

"I'll try to push from down here," Charlie says.

"And I'll — oof! — pull," you say.

You pull until you're red in the face and your arms are shaking. But the wooden slab hasn't moved a centimetre!

Could it be stuck on something? You glance around — and notice a heavy bull's hoof resting on one corner of the slab.

Your eyes travel slowly up the bull's leg. Past the heavy body. The eagle's wings. And on to the lion's head.

The beast stares down at you. You've never heard of lions laughing before, but that's what this one seems to be doing.

Slowly, the beast paces forward. And you have nowhere to run, no walls to hide behind.

Oh, well. It seems your luck was bad after all. But you were right about one thing.

You stayed to help — and that *was* final!

THE END

You swallow hard. "Go for it!" you command.

Tex Loudsnore hits a button. Streaks of blue lightning crawl along the barrel of the unconfrabulator. You close your eyes and stand absolutely still.

Hey! You thought that having your atoms destroyed would hurt. Instead, you feel light. Incredibly light. As if the slightest breath could blow you away.

You open your eyes to discover that Tex Loudsnore's laboratory has gone! Instead, you're floating among tiny, bright spots that look like stars. They glow brilliantly, red, yellow, blue, against the solid blackness.

Giggling, you swoop upwards. Multicoloured stars twirl around you. Higher and higher you go, until the coloured stars blur into a bright, harsh glare.

You don't feel weightless now, but heavy. Clumsy.

Staggering around, you grab on to . . . a door handle! You stumble into a tiny shop packed with vacuum cleaners. An old man with long grey hair grabs you by the arm as you almost fall.

"You okay, kid?" he asks.

Stagger over to PAGE 45.

Milo is ranting as you, Cammie and Jack sneak up on him.

"I didn't do all this for fun, you know!" the pumpkin-faced little man yells. "You're all down here for a very serious reason, and I want you to — YOW!"

Milo yells in shock as the three of you pile on to him. For a little guy, he's surprisingly strong. Maybe he gets his muscles from shifting around those huge boxes of comic books.

But, strong or not, there are more of you than there are of him.

It's a short, sharp battle. But in the end Jack has Milo's right arm, Cammie holds down his left, and you're perched on his chest.

"You did it!" one of the captive kids cheers. "You got Milo!"

Proceed in triumph to PAGE 108.

These dirty, weird-looking kids know more about this maze than you do. "I'll go with you guys," you decide.

"Fine," Cammie replies. "Follow us."

They lead you quickly through the maze. You're more lost than ever, now.

They yank you back when you reach a doorway. Jack raises a finger to his lips — the "be quiet" sign. You don't understand why. It sounds as if somebody is using a chain-saw on the other side.

But as you tiptoe through, you find the noise doesn't come from a machine. It comes from a pile of bandages on the floor.

No, wait. Those bandages are wrapped around a body.

Eek! A mummy!

And the mummy isn't dead — it's snoring!

Jack steps right over the sleeping creature. So does Cammie. They both beckon to you. The mummy makes weird gargling noises as you go to step over it. You're shaking so badly, your toe pokes the creature right in the side.

The snores stop. Withered eyelids open. Dried-out eyes like black raisins glare up at you!

Get out of there to PAGE 60!

I'm ahead of them, you think. And I'm good at hide-and-seek.

On tiptoe, you sneak through the maze. At last, you find a little room with only one doorway. It's hidden behind some old sheets of plywood. They'll never find you here!

But in just a few minutes, you hear an odd noise. It sounds like someone sniffling. Trying not to cry.

As the sound gets louder, you realize it's not someone sniffling, but someone *sniffing*!

A weird, humped shadow appears in the doorway. It looks like a dog, sniffing out a trail. No! It's a shaggy-headed boy, crawling along with his nose on the floor. Jack!

A chill trickles down your spine.

A second later, Jack and Cammie block the door.

Turn to PAGE 109.

126

You figure you should let Dr Doof finish the scene. It'll give him time to calm down. Then you'll be able to talk to him quietly.

You're sure you'll be able to convince him to help you!

"Let's go on with the fight, Doc," you suggest.

"Okay," the villain says. "Since we've already trashed the script, we'll have to fake it. But make it look good. Rev up your wings."

You start your wings buzzing. Dr Doof suddenly leaps back.

"My grip!" he roars. "How did you break my grip?"

I didn't, you think. *He let me go, the big phoney!*

What a cheat these fight scenes are!

You buzz around Dr Doof. He shouts threats while zapping blast-bolts at you — and missing.

"Okay. Get ready for the old A-233!" Doof whispers.

What's the old A-233? you wonder frantically.

The next thing you know, Dr Doof grabs you by the ankles!

What is *the old A-233? Find out on PAGE 91!*

You roll, bounce — even tumble in a somersault. Then there's *nothing* underneath you!

You shoot past the end of the metal slide and slam into a plywood wall. Then you thud down on to a concrete floor. "Ooof!" you groan. That hurt!

On your hands and knees, you try to climb back up the slide that used to be a stairway. But it's too steep and slippery. You just slither to the bottom again.

Trying to stay calm, you gaze round. You're in a small, shadowy room. Its walls are made of plywood. An opening leads to a plywood hallway, lit by a single bulb.

You walk down the hall. After a few metres, it turns. You find yourself in another little room. This one has three doorways. You choose the right-hand one — to find yet another hall. That one zigzags to two more rooms, then a four-way intersection of corridors.

"What's going on?" you mutter. "I feel like a rat in a maze!"

Turn to PAGE 47.

You'll go with Bob. After all, he saved you from the lion-bull-eagle monster. He knows what he's doing.

"Everybody for Bob's route, raise your hand," Russell calls.

You raise your hand. So do Dan and Alicia. Bob's short cut wins! Russell seems annoyed, but he doesn't say anything.

As you file along Bob's route, you notice that the walls of the maze are covered in grey gunk. It looks like mould. In some places there are piles of it on the floor.

"Have you ever seen this stuff before?" Russell asks Bob.

The other boy shakes his head. "No, and we shouldn't take any chances with it. Nobody touch the walls."

The stuff has a sharp, peppery smell. Your nose twitches as you move into a room where it coats the walls thickly.

It's too much. You can't help yourself. "AAAAAH-*CHOOO*!"

Your sneeze blows a clump of the mould loose from the walls. It swirls around you in a grey cloud.

But it doesn't act like any cloud you've ever seen. Instead of spreading out, it gathers *in,* circling around you and your friends.

Then the cloud breaks into five separate clouds. One for each of you!

Hold your nose and turn to PAGE 111.

Huge jaws snap hungrily just centimetres below your feet. But then you're safe on the other side of the wall. The patchwork creature roars again. It clomps off to the right.

You stare at the kid who helped you. He's bigger than you are, and older.

"Wh-who are you?" you babble. "What are you doing here?"

He grins. "It's a long story. To start with, my name is Bob."

You introduce yourself, but he's not really listening. "That lion-thing knows its way through this maze. It's going to find us if we stick around. What do you say we get out of here?"

Sounds like a great idea to you.

Bob starts leading you through the maze. "There's more of us trapped down here," he explains. "We've got a kind of camp set up."

He gives you a long stare. "I think everyone will be glad to see you," he announces. "Very glad."

March along to PAGE 39.

Nervously, you climb into the metal box. Tex Loudsnore slams the lid closed.

You lie there in darkness. Suddenly you're surrounded by a blinding light, like a camera flash. Then Loudsnore opens the box and helps you out.

"Your story seems to check out," he admits. "According to my readings, your atoms don't belong in this universe."

"Can you figure out a way to send me back?" you ask.

Loudsnore's smile is evil. "Maybe — just maybe! And if I do it right, I may get rid of Super-Doer for ever! Every other time I kill him, he comes back to life later."

"How will you do it?" you ask, a little alarmed.

"To escape from this dimension, every atom of you — and of Super-Doer — must be destroyed," Loudsnore declares.

Your teeth chatter as you repeat, "D-d-destroyed?"

Loudsnore nods. "That will free you from this comic — and me from Super-Doer!" He grabs your arm. "Just stand here in front of the unconfrabulator — and *don't move*!"

To try this route home, go to PAGE 122.

To try to escape before your atoms get destroyed, go to PAGE 96.

"I'm not going to hang around like an idiot!" you fume.

You step through the opening. Now, which way did Bob go?

There's yet another hallway. At the far end is a room.

As you scout around, you realize that this room is different. The walls are the same old plywood. But there's a trapdoor in the middle of the concrete floor!

Your heart beats faster. Could it be the way out?

You've got to investigate! The door is made of wood, with a big metal handle. You grab hold and heave.

Get on down to PAGE 110!

132

"Hey, lighten up," you complain. "I mean, I *told* Wolfen-bean he would turn into an inkblot. The writing was on the wall!"

Y's Guys aren't laughing. You try again.

"Uh — how about if we change his name to Spot?" you suggest.

Whoops. Bad joke.

"Get that kid!" the Fighting Vegetable shrieks.

Y's Guys hurl themselves at you.

As you sink under the attack, you think sadly, why did I have to be such a wise guy?

THE END

You stretch and stretch. But you can't grab your ankle in your hand.

"Sorry, you fail the test," Russell says. "You'll have to go."

Go? This nerdy-looking guy wants you to face this dangerous maze alone?

You're furious! You argue, shout, then plead. But Bob and Russell won't take you to their hideout.

"Fine!" you yell at last. "I can make it on my own. I've done all right so far."

You stomp off. You're so mad, you aren't paying attention to where you're going. And you're making lots of noise.

Still fuming, you step through a doorway and trip over something. It's long, cool and scaly.

Oops! You just bumped into the snake-creature again!

Stumble to PAGE 41.

The hairy hand of Professor Y points right at you!

"Um, ah. . ." It's not the smoothest answer. But it's the best you can do when your mouth is dry with terror.

But Professor Y's hand swings past you to point at Stinky Stanley. "No!" the professor cries. "It's *you*! No — wait!"

He turns to Jean Greene. "Now my powers point to you!"

Something very strange is going on. . .

The professor goes from one Y's Guy to another. "And you! And you!" His voice drips with horror. "Great Googly Moogly! You're *all* from outside this universe!"

You stare at the other superheroes. Could this be true? Could they *all* be kids who were sucked into comics?

"Death to the invaders!" Professor Y snarls. He flings deadly hair balls at all of you. You've seen these things in the comic — they can choke you to death!

Turn to PAGE 53.

You might as well go for it.

"Yes," you answer boldly, "I *could* do better!"

"Yeah, right," Milo scoffs. "Okay, close your eyes and think of the scariest creature you can."

You close your eyes, remembering a horrifying creature from a book you read. A GOOSEBUMPS book. The creature — King Jellyjam — was a huge, quivering balloon of purple slime. Its watery yellow eyes peered over a blob of a nose running with white goo. It had big, rubbery lips that blubbered and burped. It smelled like dirty sweat socks filled with rotten fish — or worse!

And its gross, gooey body was always sweating. Not just plain sweat. King Jellyjam sweated live snails!

You open your eyes to tell Milo about the creature.

Oh, no. This is really bad!

Milo is changing — mutating. Into King Jellyjam!

Shiver to PAGE 84.

The solid steel feels like Silly Putty under your fist! You keep pounding until you tear a hole through the door.

Then you use both hands to rip an opening large enough to walk through. You step into the mad scientist's laboratory.

You recognize Tex Loudsnore easily from the comics. He's tall, skinny and he doesn't have any hair. Instead, the top half of his head is made of a gleaming chrome dome. He's Tex Loudsnore, the man with the pop-top head! Tex Loudsnore, villain and monster-maker!

"Super-Doer!" he snarls. "I don't know how you found me. But my latest invention can handle even you!"

The mad scientist hefts a test-tube in his hand. Then he throws it at you! Can you catch it?

To find out, hold a thirty-centimetre ruler straight up, with your thumb and forefinger on the bottom at the zero mark. Open your fingers to let the ruler drop. Then catch it again.

If you catch the ruler between the zero mark and the twenty-centimetre mark, go to PAGE 114.

If you catch the ruler between the twenty-centimetre mark and the thirty-centimetre mark, go to PAGE 105.

If you don't catch the ruler at all . . . try again!

When you wake up again, the first thing you notice is that you're really cold.

The second thing you notice is that you're lying on a metal table. Surrounded by people in white coats.

You blink. "What's up?" you ask. "Where am I?"

"The kid's alive," a man cries. "It's a medical miracle!"

As it turns out, the people in white coats are scientists, studying the ice in Antarctica. Imagine their surprise when they found *you* — frozen into one of the icebergs. Alive!

No one knows how you got all the way to Antarctica. Or how you stayed alive inside your ice coating. For the next two weeks, you're poked and prodded by dozens of doctors.

Finally they give up and send you home.

That's when the newspapers and TV stations start calling. They all want the life story of the Icekid.

And they offer you big bucks!

Soon you have so much money you don't know how to spend it all. Well, actually, you've got a few ideas.

Starting with a trip to a comic-book shop. . .

THE END

R.L.Stine

Reader beware, you're in for a scare!

These terrifying tales will send shivers up your spine:

1 Welcome to Dead House
2 Say Cheese and Die!
3 Stay Out of the Basement
4 The Curse of the Mummy's Tomb
5 Monster Blood
6 Let's Get Invisible!
7 Night of the Living Dummy
8 The Girl Who Cried Monster
9 Welcome to Camp Nightmare
10 The Ghost Next Door
11 The Haunted Mask
12 Piano Lessons Can Be Murder
13 Be Careful What You Wish For
14 The Werewolf of Fever Swamp
15 You Can't Scare Me!
16 One Day at HorrorLand
17 Why I'm Afraid of Bees
18 Monster Blood II
19 Deep Trouble
20 Go Eat Worms
21 Return of the Mummy
22 The Scarecrow Walks at Midnight
23 Attack of the Mutant
24 My Hairiest Adventure
25 A Night in Terror Tower
26 The Cuckoo Clock of Doom
27 Monster Blood III
28 Ghost Beach
29 Phantom of the Auditorium

30 It Came From Beneath the Sink!
31 Night of the Living Dummy II
32 The Barking Ghost
33 The Horror at Camp Jellyjam
34 Revenge of the Garden Gnomes
35 A Shocker on Shock Street
36 The Haunted Mask II
37 The Headless Ghost
38 The Abominable Snowman of Pasadena
39 How I Got My Shrunken Head
40 Night of the Living Dummy III
41 Bad Hare Day
42 Egg Monsters From Mars
43 The Beast From the East
44 Say Cheese and Die – Again!
45 Ghost Camp
46 How to Kill a Monster
47 Legend of the Lost Legend
48 Attack of the Jack-O'-Lanterns
49 Vampire Breath
50 Calling All Creeps!
51 Beware, the Snowman
52 How I Learned to Fly
53 Chicken Chicken
54 Don't Go To Sleep!
55 The Blob That Ate Everyone
56 The Curse of Camp Cold Lake
57 My Best Friend is Invisible
58 Deep Trouble II
59 The Haunted School
60 Werewolf Skin
61 I Live in Your Basement
62 Monster Blood IV